STRIKE DEEP

Anthony
North
The Dial Press
NEW YORK · 1974

STRIKE
DEEP

Designed by Paula Wiener
Manufactured in the United States of America
Second printing, 1974

Library of Congress Cataloging in Publication Data

North, Anthony.
Strike deep.

I. Title.
PZ4.N8565St [PS3564.068] 813'.5'4 74-4145
ISBN 0-8037-8338-8

To my wife

I want to thank Dr. Edward X. O'Brien,
Dr. Sarah Ann Mishkin, and Robert Dall for
technical advice and for information without which
I would have had to write another book altogether.

DECEMBER 26–
DECEMBER 27

The Proposition

1.

Lee Ackridge was two blocks from home when a sudden flurry of snowflakes struck his face and melted on his skin. For the first time all morning, he looked up and saw that the grimy New York City sky was even grayer than usual. Billowing over the roofs of the dark buildings, low and menacing masses of clouds rolled steadily eastward like columns of smoke. This was not just a squall, but the beginning of a storm, the initial ghostly touch of the season's first appreciable snowfall.

It figures, he thought sourly. In his current mood, even the vicissitudes of the weather struck him as personal attacks directed solely against him.

Here was one more inconvenience with which he would have to deal, one more problem to make life difficult. On Christmas, when snow was necessary and good and welcome, the weather had been crisp but sunny. Now, when there was no emotional, nostalgic, or symbolic benefit to be gained from it, the snow had come. Soon, the sidewalks would be slushy and icy, the streets all but impassable. Getting from one place to another would become a sloppy ordeal.

He wiped the melted flakes off his face and cursed under his breath. Frosty plumes swirled in the air ahead of him.

At the apartment house on Twentieth Street, he took the outside steps two at a time and, at the top, pulled open the battered front door.

Over the last three years, he had gotten accustomed to the building, and he normally went in and out without noticing the shabbiness. However, because everything was going wrong today and because he was angry with the world, he noticed. He noticed too damned much. The steps which he had negotiated in pairs were cracked and hoved up, the concrete crumbling out of the corners. Scarred and badly weathered, the foyer door was centered with cracked glass which had been crudely repaired with strips of black plastic electrician's tape. The foyer itself was dirty and dimly lit, and several of the mailboxes had been prized open and bent out of shape.

He searched his pockets, realizing for the first time that he had left this morning without taking his key. He pressed the button under the label which read APARTMENT F—ACKRIDGE, HOFFMAN.

The intercom crackled with Carrie's voice. The static was so heavy that she was totally unintelligible.

"It's Lee!" he shouted. It was necessary to shout if she were going to understand him over the bad sound system.

The buzzer rang.

He grabbed the handle of the inner door and entered the downstairs hall. He walked up six flights to the third floor, painfully aware that the stairwell was not much warmer than the winter streets outside.

Carrie was waiting for him at the apartment door on the third floor. She smiled tentatively.

As usual when she was at home, she wore a pair of old, faded jeans and one of his T-shirts, but to him she was no less beautiful than she would have been in an evening gown. Her hair was glossy and thick, tumbling in soft amber curves to her shoulders. It framed a face which belonged in television commercials for Pepsi Cola. Although she was twenty-three, she could easily have passed for a sixteen-year-old ingenue, wide-eyed and fresh of spirit. Her clear, dark blue eyes were complemented by a complexion as creamy and flawless as the airbrushed bosom and backside of the latest Playmate. Her body was not sufficiently busty to match the fantasy ideal that would have landed her in the better men's magazines, but it was, to Lee, decidedly erotic. She was slender, with small high breasts and a pinched waist, boyish hips, yet a firm round behind. Her long legs brought her to within four inches of his own five-eleven. In jeans and T-shirt, she was more desirable than most women could be even in abbreviated cocktail dresses.

He knew he was fortunate in having her. No matter how bad the morning had been and no matter how depressing the apartment house was, the day would not be a total loss if Carrie shared it with him. She could make all the difference. Indeed, for the last year, she *had* made all the difference. She had kept him out of the worst of the gloom and self-pity which had preoccupied him ever since his return to the States from Southeast Asia nearly four years ago.

His optimism suddenly flipped over. Sure, she had made a big difference. She certainly made life easier. But how long would she stay with a man who woke screaming from nightmares at least once every night and needed to have her nurse him as if he were a child? How long *could* she stay with a man who was, nine times out of ten, incapable of making love to her? With his scarred face and his worm's nest of neuroses, could he honestly hope to hold onto her for more than a few additional weeks—or days?

As he came up to the door, she stood on her toes and kissed him. She shivered at the touch of his cold hands, pulled back, and said, "It must be hell out there."

He nodded.

"Snowing?"

"Yeah."

He stripped out of his coat and dropped it on a tattered easy chair as he crossed the room.

In the kitchen, as he pulled the top off a can of Budweiser, she said, "Bad news?"

"What do you think?"

He was unable to look at her. He did not want to tell her that as bad as things were they would still get worse.

"Lee. . . ?"

He took a long drink of beer, realizing that what he really needed was something to warm him. Then he thought of Templeton up at the Veterans' Administration office from which he had just come, and he decided that he needed to be picked up more than warmed up.

"Bad news, I guess." She frowned. "But that doesn't mean you have to take it out on me."

He sat down at the cheap formica table. "I'm sorry." He was not able to consciously hurt her feelings. His sullenness had been a defense against the rest of the world, not against her.

"I'll bet you haven't had breakfast or lunch." She was tactfully avoiding any talk of the VA and Mr. Peter Templeton, giving him the right to choose the best moment for that. "Sandwich?"

"I suppose."

"Bologna, white cheese, lettuce, a slice of tomato. . . ?"

"O.K. But I'll get it."

She shook her head. Her yellow hair trembled delightfully.

"No. You stay there. No one can call you a male chauvinist just because you let me fix one sandwich for you."

"You do too much for me."

"I haven't done enough," she said.

He had finished the beer by the time the sandwich was ready, and she opened a second can for him. She opened another for herself, although she drank from a glass.

"What kind of day have you had?" he asked, between bites.

He was sitting in the chair nearest the refrigerator, and he had turned it slightly away from the table. Whichever of the other three chairs she sat in, she would be unable to see the half of his face which was twisted by scar tissue. She had told him not to be self-conscious. She said she did not find him ugly or think of him as disfigured. She barely noticed the scars. Nevertheless, he hid the right side of his face at meal times and whenever they made love.

"I didn't get up until ten o'clock," she said. She worked in the art department of a publishing house which had offices in mid-town Manhattan, where she was given the day off after both Thanksgiving and Christmas. "I've been listening to the radio and reading."

He ate the last of the sandwich, enjoyed several swallows of beer. Leaning back in his chair, he was finally able to talk about the VA and Templeton. "They're cutting off the support payments."

"Altogether?"

"Yes."

"Who'd you talk to?"

"Who else?"

"Templeton."

"Yes."

"Appeal," she said. "Try to go over his head."

"It wouldn't matter."

"Templeton's a bastard," she said.

"True. But they're all like that, or at least they stick together. His decision would be upheld."

She sipped her beer. Her pretty face was now deeply lined. "You showed him Dr. Slatvik's letter?"

"Sure."

"What did he say about that?"

Lee shrugged. "It didn't impress him."

She slapped the top of the table with one delicate palm. "Dammit, you *deserve* a disability pension."

He was always amazed that she could continue to believe in the innate fairness of life regardless of what happened to her and to those around her. Before Carrie was born, her father deserted his family. She had never seen him. Her mother was a borderline alcoholic who was completely irresponsible and given to associating with equally unreliable men who did no better by her than Carrie's father had done. They had existed on the edge of poverty all of Carrie's childhood. When she was nineteen, her fiancee had been killed in a training mishap only four weeks after he had been drafted into the Army . . . Yet Carrie expected only good fortune and was helplessly surprised by every bad turn in her life. And she was absolutely enraged when she perceived an absence of justice in the workings of fate.

"You deserve it," she repeated.

He fetched another beer from the refrigerator.

"Want a second round?" he asked.

"No. I still have some."

Returning to his chair, he kept the scarred half of his face turned away from her.

"Exactly what did Templeton say?"

"Do we have to go into that?"

"I'd like to hear it."

He sighed. When he spoke, he quoted Templeton: "The

United States government will pay a disability pension only if the serviceman's injuries, sustained during his tour of duty, continue to render him less employable than he otherwise might have been."

"Well, you've certainly—"

Lee held up one hand to silence her. "Plastic surgery, which was completely paid for by the government, has removed sixty-five per cent of the scars from the right side of my face." He was still quoting Templeton, but now he had personalized the pronouns. "I may not be a movie star, but neither am I repulsively ugly. So what if thirty-five per cent of the scars aren't amenable to plastic surgery? So what if half my face is left expressionless because of paralyzed muscles?" He was no longer quoting anyone. His voice grew more bitter with each word. "So what if my skin on that side feels like cardboard? At least I'm not deaf in either ear or blind in either eye. What on earth have I got to complain about? Look how fortunate I've been!"

They were both quiet for a while.

The tiny kitchen, brightened only by the winter light that came through two narrow windows, seemed to close in on them.

At last she said, "Psychological disability. For God's sake, what about that?" She made a fist with one hand, and the slim bands of muscle tensed under the softness of that slender arm.

"Templeton has the answer."

"It can't be very sensible."

"There's some truth in it," Lee admitted. "Damn little, but some. He says it's apparent that whatever psychological problems I have aren't serious enough to interfere with my employment suitability. After all, he says, I'm attending Columbia University, carrying a heavier than average student course load. I'm maintaining a 3.5 grade average. If I can do so well as a law student, think of what a glowing future I have as a lawyer. I don't need their help, he says. Any psychological problems I have are, he says, evidently personal and in no way related to my ability to earn a living."

If Templeton had been in the room, Carrie would have lunged for him, and the world would have contained one less bureaucrat. "Who the hell is he to say that?"

"I don't know. Maybe he's getting a degree in psychology from some correspondence school."

She didn't think that was funny. "What about your tuition?"

"Oh, the G.I. Bill will continue to pay most of that. And I'll even get something toward books."

"What about food? Rent? A thousand other little bills?"

He turned and faced her directly, forgetting to hide his scars. In the dim December light, the right side of his face seemed to be slightly rippled, as if she were viewing it through several inches of water. It was dead, slack. That side of his mouth was immobile, as if the last inch of his lips had been painted in place. He smiled sarcastically with the good half of his mouth. "Templeton is confident that I can arrange for a part-time job that won't get in the way of my studies. He even offered to help me find one."

Her eyes shone like a deer's eyes in the semi-darkness, but her mood was that of the wolf. "He *knows* you've got a heavy class schedule. Doesn't he understand that Monday through Thursday you're in class all morning and afternoon—and for another three hours on Friday? Doesn't he realize you have to spend four or five hours a day studying? And all Saturday in the library?"

"Yeah, sure he does," Lee said. Then he tried to amuse her, to dispel her gloom in a way quite like she usually dispelled his own. He did an imitation of a slightly punchy, would-be champion prizefighter from an old movie: "But Mr. Templeton has a *whole lot* of confidence in me. He thinks I'll go all the way, right up to the top!"

"So do I," she said, unwilling to be amused. Her voice became soft without losing the strength of anger. "I have more confidence in you than a hundred Templetons ever could. But you aren't Superman." Suddenly, as she thought of something else, the softness left her voice, and she was full of anger again. "What about the weekly sessions with Dr. Slatvik?"

He lifted the can of beer and took a long drink, temporarily avoiding giving her another unpleasant bit of news. "There's that, too," he said at last.

"They won't pay for a psychotherapist anymore?"

"Not for Slatvik, anyway."

"What do you mean?"

"Templeton says their budget for that sort of thing has been slashed. So . . . they'll only provide psychiatric care through an Army doctor. He says he'll gladly assign me to someone here in New York."

"But Slatvik's been on your case for nearly three years. He knows it, knows you. And what will this Army quack be, a psychotherapist or a psychoanalyst? An analyst wouldn't be any good for you. Besides, any psychiatrist who's making a career of the Army has to have bad problems of his own."

"It doesn't matter," Lee said, though it mattered very much. "I've already decided I won't go to another doctor. To hell with doctors." He grinned lopsidedly to show her how little Templeton's decision had affected him. "My grandmother used to treat herself for the common ailments, and she never died by her own hand. I guess I can treat myself for the more complicated sicknesses."

"*Damn them!*" she said fiercely. She got up and went to the nearest window, looked out at the swiftly falling snow and the gray city which the snow was gradually painting.

For a few seconds the apartment was silent. Then the street

noises drifted in: the hollow rumble of cars and trucks, the mournful distant cry of a police siren . . .

He got up and stood behind her. He put his arms around her waist and drew her back against him. A clean, shampoo smell wafted up from her thick hair.

"It won't do any good to brood about it," he said.

"And it won't do any harm, either," she said.

"Brooding just makes for more depression. There's nothing to be done, nothing we can change." He looked past her head at the snowflakes drifting by the window. "This morning, I realized there's no use blaming Templeton. He's not responsible for the government's policies. He's the bureaucratic arm we have to wrestle with, so we tend to think it's all his fault. But he has no choice. He's only doing what he's told to do."

"You're too damned reasonable," she said. "We've got to make plans."

"Got any ideas?"

Her back still to him, she said, "We'll give up things, become regular Spartans. We'll learn to live on my salary."

"Then we'll have to give up food," he said.

She sighed. "I just don't know . . ."

"*I'll* get a job," he said. "I'll cut down on my course load and take an extra year to finish the degree."

"No!" She was adamant. "If you delay it, you might never finish." She pulled out of his arms, turned and faced him.

"Look," he said, "the only alternative is to borrow. But there's no bank that'll lend living money to an unemployed, disfigured student with a history of psychiatric treatment. And who else is there? My father?"

He had never been close to his father. The old man had only visited him once in all the time he was in the hospital, and then there had been an argument about the war and current politics. They could find no neutral ground anymore.

As if exhausted, she leaned against him. "Hold me."

He put his arms around her again. He realized that this was a time for making love. But he also realized that this would not be one of those rare occasions when he would be capable of it. He just held her.

2.

Lee stared at his face in the age-streaked bathroom mirror and tried to remember how he had once looked: curly brown hair, a firm jawline, square chin, ruddy complexion, freckles. He had been a regular Jack Armstrong with All-American good looks. He had lost precisely half those looks to scar tissue. He was not Jack Armstrong anymore.

Be thankful you still have both arms and legs, he thought. He knew other men who'd lost more than he had. He stood five-eleven, weighed a natural one-seventy, was lean and muscular. He had both his eyes. It could be worse.

Usually, by making himself confront his wounds, he could generate anger, a fierce desire for revenge which snapped him out of his depression. Today, that approach did not work. If there were no way to gain revenge against the mammoth, faceless bureaucracy of the government, why waste energy nurturing that useless desire?

The downstairs buzzer rang.

Wanting to be alone to consider their problems, Carrie had gone out for a walk. She would not be back this early.

Lee switched off the bathroom light, went down the hall to the apartment door where he used the intercom. "Who's there?"

A meaningless wash of static was the only answer. It could have been a junkie saying, "Man, I need money for a fix, and I'm ready to kill for it."

More likely, it *was* Carrie. She had probably forgotten her key, just as he had done earlier.

He thumbed the lock release for the downstairs entrance, then pulled open the apartment door and stepped into the corridor to face the head of the stairs. There were heavy footsteps coming up. It was not Carrie, but a man. Really a junkie after all?

"Ackridge, you're a sorry sight," the visitor said, coming off the top of the steps onto the third floor.

Lee squinted, blinked. "Doug? My *God!* Doug!"

Douglas Powell, the only close friend he had made while in the Army, closed the space between them and gripped Lee by the shoulders. He was six-three, four inches taller than Lee, but he weighed only a pound or two more than did the smaller man. He was exceptionally hard and stringy. In the war, the other men had called him Wire, partly because of the way he could coil up and hide his long frame in a surprisingly small patch of ground cover. His hands were made for playing basketball, and they felt enormous on Lee's shoulders.

"You look like a whipped dog," Powell said.

Lee laughed.

"I'm serious."

"Does it really show?"

Powell's quick, sharp voice became somber. "You want to tell me all about it?"

Punching playfully at the lanky man's stomach, Lee said, "You come on strong, don't you?"

"That's my style."

"You're here three seconds, and already you're offering to guide me through the shoals of life."

Powell spread his long arms wide. "Who better?"

"I can think of several," Lee said. "But, Jesus, I'm just getting used to the idea you're here. What's the occasion?"

Powell grinned winningly. He had a long, dark face with tea-colored eyes that were sunk deeply under a broad forehead. His nose was a formidable beak that hooked out above contrastingly thin lips. His teeth were perfect for grinning: square and white; they were the ideal testament to the desirability of making regular visits to an expensive orthodontist in one's youth. "The occasion?" Powell asked. "Come inside with me, have a drink, and I'll tell you." Then he pushed Lee into the apartment, slamming the door behind them.

"A beer?" Lee asked.

"Two," Powell said. "One for each hand."

They went through the narrow, cluttered living room into the even smaller kitchen.

"Didn't you pay your light bill?" Powell asked. "Or do you like living in the dark?"

"Before you showed up," Lee said, "I was in the mood for darkness." He reached for the light switch over the kitchen sink.

"No, no!" Powell said, quickly. "I like it. It's kind of relaxing, with the music and all."

In the other room, the radio was still tuned to an FM channel. The music of the Living Strings and the lengthening late-afternoon shadows were all around them, two intangible security blankets. Lee dropped his hand from the switch without flicking on the lights.

Powell took off his heavy, knee-length topcoat and draped it over the back of a kitchen chair, sat down at the formica table while Lee got the beers.

Sitting with his back at one of the kitchen windows, more silhouetted than illuminated, Powell sipped at his two beers and said, "Now, what has you so down?"

"That's not your worry," Lee said.

"Like hell it isn't! You saved my life. Least I can do is listen to your problems now."

"It went two ways in Nam," Lee said.

"And it goes two ways here, too." Powell raised a can of beer, tilted his head back, and nearly drained away a whole twelve-ounce serving in one long, gulping swallow. Sighing happily, he said, "Later on, I've got some problems of my own I want to tell you all about."

"Oh?"

"You first."

Because he knew that Powell could be stubborn when he had his mind set on something, and because it was clear that Powell had his mind set on listening to his friend's troubles, Lee told him about Templeton and the VA, about the discontinuance of his disability pension, the financial problems, the loss of psychiatric care, about everything except his enduring impotency which was strictly his and Carrie's business . . .

All through the recitation, Lee had the inexplicable feeling that the other man was secretly pleased by his misfortunes. But that was impossible. Douglas Powell was no sadist. And they were close friends . . .

"Then Carrie moved in?" Powell asked.

"Didn't you know?"

"I haven't seen you since before Christmas last year. You'd met her at a Thanksgiving Day party, and you were dating her then."

"She moved in a week after I saw you, almost a full year ago."

"Happy?"

"She's about all I've got to be happy with."

"More than I've got," Powell said. It was not characteristic of him to admit to depression or defeat of any sort. He gave Lee this one quick glimpse of loneliness, then closed up. He chugged down his second beer and wiped his lips with the back of his hand.

"Want another?"

"Naturally." When he had the third beer in his hand, Powell said, "I just chucked the idea of being an architect."

"You dropped out of school?"

"Again," Powell admitted.

"How many does this make?"

"Five schools and four careers since I got back from Nam four years ago," Powell said. "First I tried computer design and technology, then business administration, medicine, architecture . . . I'm twenty-six years old, and I'm thinking of making a career as a professional dropout." He grinned without humor, showing lots of white teeth and looking chillingly like a hungry, carnivorous beast.

"What's wrong, Doug?"

"I don't know. Since Nam, I can't seem to settle down."

Lee nodded. "I guess it scarred both of us."

After taking another long drink of beer, Powell slammed the can down on the table. "But by God, I'm on to something now!"

"What's that?" Lee asked, watching him closely and wondering about his quick changes of mood.

Powell looked around at the tiny kitchen, through the archway at the dark, musty living room. "In one way, I feel terrible about what's happened to you. It upsets me that this is the best you can afford. I feel just awful about Templeton and the VA and all the rest of it. But in another way—I'm pleased."

It had not been his imagination, then. Powell *had* been secretly delighted when he had heard of the problems, the worries, the long list of disappointments. But why?

Powell answered that unspoken question. "As rotten as it sounds, I'm glad they've tramped all over you, because it makes you all the more ready to accept a little proposition that I've come here to make."

"Proposition?"

Powell smiled. It was still a somehow lupine, threatening expression.

"What do you mean?" Lee asked.

"Money."

"You mean a business proposition?" But Lee was uneasily certain that Powell meant nothing of the sort.

"Business? In a way it is, I guess."

Ackridge waited a full minute. Then: "Well?"

Doug Powell hunched over the table, folded his big hands around a beer can as if he would crush it between his palms. So little light was coming through the windows now that he was hardly more than a shadow. "Lee . . ." He hesitated, then spoke in a careful, measured tone of voice, abandoning his usual rapid-fire delivery. "How would you like to be a millionaire?"

Ackridge just looked at him.

"How would you like to be a millionaire?" Powell repeated. "No more money crises, no worries at all."

Lee broke out laughing. "Great! Sure!"

Powell grimaced. "You *can* be," he said seriously. "And so can I. Soon. Both of us."

The kitchen seemed to grow colder, as if someone had opened a window and was letting in the winter wind. Lee had not seen an intensity like that in Powell's eyes since he had been in Nam.

"Doug, what is this?"

"I've come across . . . something," Powell said, enigmatically. He shifted in his seat. Now he was in complete darkness. "I need a partner. I need someone I can trust with my life. I don't know who else that would be but you."

"And it involves a million dollars?"

"Several million," Powell said.

They were both silent for a while.

At last Lee said, "It's illegal, isn't it?"

"To be trite but truthful," Powell said, "they'd throw away the key."

3.

Lee turned on the light over the kitchen stove; he no longer liked the darkness. "Maybe I should tell you to shut up right now," he said. "We could have another beer, and then you could go."

"That's up to you," Powell said. "But you'd always be sorry you didn't at least listen to me."

"What if I listen and then decide I want no part of it?"

"You aren't obligated."

He stared at Powell and tried to read his long, hard face; but he found that he did not know the right language. There was a noticeable but unidentifiable foreign element in Doug. He was not the same man whom Lee had known in the war.

"Well?" Powell asked.

"Several million dollars . . . Where, besides a mint, do they let that kind of money out where it can be grabbed?"

"Is that just an idle question—or does it mean you want to hear what I've got?" Powell asked, leaning forward again. His quick movements and easygoing manner had disappeared. He moved slowly yet with an aura of energy and power, like a lizard in cold weather.

Lee watched him and thought about him and tried to find a handle on all of this. Why was Douglas Eugene Powell, of all people, proposing robbery? Or hijacking? Or whatever crime he had in mind? Powell had everything going for him. He didn't *need* to take what he wanted. He could have it handed to him, just for the asking.

His mother, Loretta Collinswood Powell, raised in the upper-class Dixie tradition of charm, grace, social generosity, and genteel bigotry, was a pretty but silly southern belle who had produced no other children. Heiress to one-fourth of her family's real estate interests, she was no millionairess but certainly came close. Judging from what little Doug had said about her, she seemed to be a soft touch, a doting mother who would routinely provide whatever was requested.

General Norman Powell was Chairman of the Joint Chiefs of Staff. He could pull all the strings Doug might need pulled.

Doug talked about his father even less often than about his mother. When Lee and Doug had been in the Army, General Powell had not been Chairman of the Joint Chiefs. But he *had* been a general. Lee had always supposed that Doug's reluctance to talk about his family came from a desire not to brag about the general. He had always wanted to be one of the guys, nothing more. He had not been the kind of soldier who would use a relative's connections to make his own lot easier. However, whether or not he talked about his father, the general was there nonetheless, as formidable an asset to his son as was Loretta's money.

Doug did not have to steal.

Then why was he sitting here, earnest and straight-faced, talking about theft?

And why am I so damned eager to hear what he has to say? Lee suddenly wondered. If Doug's changed, so have I.

He looked at the kitchen clock. Carrie had been gone a full hour. She might be back at any moment, and she should not become involved in this, in any way. Therefore, if Powell was going to spell it out, there was no time for delay.

"Go ahead," Lee said.

Doug nodded. His voice was low and firm. It was as if time had run backwards, as if they were in Asia again, in the jungle again, discussing the strategy to use against a Cong patrol that had them pinned down in a bad position.

"The way I figure it," Powell said, "we'll net anywhere between four and six million dollars, split fifty-fifty." He sounded like a man discussing a tricky but legal stock or commodities deal. Neat, well-groomed, well-dressed, the respectable son of an honored family, he did not seem at all like a thief.

Lee shook his head. "That's too much money. It doesn't seem real."

"It'll seem damned real when you have your hands on it," Powell said, smiling.

Was he joking?

Lee stared at him again, saw that intense determination in his eyes.

"First of all," Powell said, "we wouldn't be taking cash. For one thing, it would weigh too much. For another, it would be traceable. And for a third—you're right when you say we'd have to hit a mint to pick up that much loose money." He reached in his shirt pocket, pulled out cigarettes and matches. "We'll be stealing something that's so damned valuable we'll be able to ransom it for millions."

"Wait a minute," Lee said, quickly. "Kidnapping? That's a capital offense."

Powell drew on his cigarette. "I know. I'm not crazy. It isn't kidnapping."

"Then what? An airliner full of people? That's kidnapping, too."

"Patience," Powell said, holding up one big hand, his cigarette pinched between two long fingers. "It's complicated."

Lee wanted another beer, but he knew he was near his limit and would get fuzzy-headed if he drank any more. He strained to concentrate.

"In Washington, D.C., by the Potomac River," Doug said, sounding like the voiceover on a travelogue, "stands the most closely guarded building in the world. It contains the equivalent of one armed guard for every forty feet of corridor. There are twenty-four-hour-a-day police dog patrols of the grounds. Electronic alarms and sophisticated protection systems of all sorts proliferate. You couldn't get five feet past the entrance. Neither could I . . . Yet I can steal that building's most valuable contents. The two of us can. Without ever going within a hundred miles of it."

No matter how serious Powell seemed to be, this was beginning to sound like a riddle. "We can steal from it without going near it?"

Powell smiled. "Yes."

"You're losing me. Let's stop talking generalities. What building is this?"

"The Pentagon."

Lee thought about that. Then: "Your father has offices there. I thought you said you couldn't get five feet past the door?"

"Oh, I could go in with my father. But I'd be under constant observation. I couldn't take a breath without someone noting it."

"They don't even trust the Chairman of the—"

"They trust nobody," Powell said. "But we're getting off the track. I told you we don't have to go anywhere near the place."

"O.K. I'm hooked. I want that explained. But first . . . What in the hell would we swipe from the Pentagon and ransom for millions?"

"Information."

The single word was like a bucket of ice water thrown in Lee's face. It washed away the comic book aura which had surrounded the conversation. "Jesus!"

Powell laughed.

"You want to steal classified material."

The lilting Mantovani music drifted in from the radio in the living room—odd background, Lee thought, for this sort of talk.

"Not just classified," Powell said. "I'm thinking of top of the line, eyes only, deadly important material."

"This isn't just robbery. It's treason!"

"Not at all. To be guilty of treason, we'd have to turn the stuff over to a foreign government. Naturally, to make our own government pay the ransom, we'll threaten to do just that. But we'll never really carry through on the threat."

"We're still talking in generalities," Lee said. He was sweating. His face was damp and shiny. His shirt was discolored by patches of perspiration.

Powell blew a smoke ring and tried to look relaxed. But he was clearly as taut as the tightrope he proposed to walk. "In the subbasements of the Pentagon," Powell said, again the travelogue narrator, "stands the world's largest computer system. Multigenerational and constantly updated, it has memory banks amounting to fifteen thousand magnetic drums, equivalent to 180,000,000 feet of magnetic tape, better than three billion computer words of information. At least a third of it is highly classified —and highly valuable. You following me?"

Lee nodded. "Where do you get all this? Your father?"

"Sure. The only two things he ever talks about are football and the Pentagon."

Whatever the nature of his plan, he was clearly excited by it. Thus far, Lee Ackridge was only frightened.

Powell continued: "For the convenience of those who use the Defense Department computer, all the data has been accumulated under fifty simplified categories. In those fifty categories is every salient fact about this country's military preparedness. If an enemy were to tap those data reserves for even a fraction of the classified material they contain, the world balance of power would shift overnight. If *substantial* data were obtained by the wrong people, the certain and swift decline of the United States would follow."

"War?"

His hands betraying the nervousness which he otherwise hid so well, Powell crushed his cigarette in a glass ashtray which Lee had given him, and then he quickly lit another. "An enemy in possession of this stuff would probably find war unnecessary. Imagine what another nation could do if it possessed our own records of the work of Army and CIA assassination squads in South America. We could be humiliated, discredited before the world community . . . You see, this information would be a weapon quite different from battlefield advantage."

"In the wrong hands," Lee said, "stuff like that could change the course of history." That didn't sound the least bit melodramatic, he thought. Indeed, it was an understatement. He did not yet fully comprehend what other secrets this computer might hold. But he *did* understand that they were talking about momentous things.

"But we'll see that it *doesn't* get into the wrong hands," Powell quickly assured him. "We'll only take a small part of the most classified stuff. Five or six magnetic tapes, carefully preselected data. For instance, we could get a good ransom if we held the taped files of every American weapons research program that's concerned with lasers. Imagine what Russia, China, France, or anyone else could do with the basic research paid for with hundreds of millions of American dollars. And imagine what our government would pay to have those tapes returned before any other country saw them." He took a deep drag on his cigarette and watched comprehension come slowly but relentlessly to Lee. "That's just part of it. We could steal the mag tapes that contain every U.S. contingency plan for future local and world wars. Or a complete file of the Pentagon's knowledge of scientific studies in the Soviet Union, including the names of double agents and informers who supplied the Pentagon with each datum. Despite the rumors that the cold war is over, what do you think Russia would pay for that information?"

"Good God."

"Or suppose we had mag tapes containing the code names, contact points, mail drops, false fronts, and standing orders of every CIA agent in the world, plus the real names and addresses of fully half of them. If an enemy were to get possession of all that, our international espionage network would be destroyed, and we'd need ten years to establish it again."

Lee felt hot and dizzy. "Even if there were some way you could get to this data, we'd be crazy to steal it."

"Oh?"

"If you ever got those files, and if our government ransomed them, you'd never have any peace the rest of your life. The CIA, NSA, FBI, and God knows what other agencies, would dog the case until they sank their teeth in you."

"There are safeguards," Powell insisted. "But I'll go into those later. Right now, I want you to understand that there is no doubt about my getting that data. I can do it."

"Without ever approaching the Pentagon?"

"Just as I said."

"From your *father?*"

Powell laughed. He had an engaging laugh. "Of course not! And look here, this doesn't smack of Benedict Arnold. We may *threaten* to turn the stuff over to China or Russia or Spain or *someone.* We have to make the threat if we're to get the ransom. But we'd never carry through with it. If worse comes to worst and we can't get our money, we destroy the tapes. Or mail them back."

"And how will they know we didn't copy the tapes?"

Doug crushed out his second cigarette. He turned up both palms as if to show his hands were clean. "Simple. The tape system they use is designed for security more than for efficiency. It can't be copied except with their own equipment."

Why am I still listening to this craziness, Lee wondered. Was it just curiosity that kept him from telling Powell to say no more? Curiosity? *No. I'm listening, because I haven't yet decided he can count me out.*

"If you aren't going into the Pentagon or anywhere near this computer," Lee said, "then you know someone inside who's corruptible."

"That place is full of corrupt men," Doug said. It was clear that he was thinking chiefly of his father. "But no one could sneak anything off the computer floor, let alone out of the building." He lighted a third cigarette. "No Defense Department employee can obtain top secret files without first getting priority security clearance. That takes time. Then he has to fill out a form requesting specific data. Then, the computer's chief programmer, a man named Ives, will get the information for him. That employee will never even touch the computer himself."

"This Ives could—"

"He submits to a search every time he leaves the computer floor," Powell said. "And there are always guards watching the operations." He started to stub out his cigarette before he had taken even a second puff; but he caught himself, reddened slightly, then continued to explain the setup. "Of those fifty data categories for classified material, none can be tapped unless the data request is prefaced by a code word that represents that category. The words change every two weeks. Only nine people —all of them with computer consoles in their offices which tap into the Pentagon system—receive booklets containing the code. Those nine are pretty much unassailable: Ives, the chief programmer who establishes the code in the first place; the President; the Vice-President; the Secretary of Defense; Chairman of the Joint Chiefs of Staff; the heads of the other three armed services; and the Pentagon's Congressional Liaison, who decides which Representatives and Senators will be made privy to how much of what particular secret material. All those men are above reproach, right? Anyone else who does not have the code words and his own personal computer link, and anyone who cannot get top security clearance, can obtain data only if it's unclassified, open to public scrutiny."

"If your father hasn't turned traitor, then the President or one of those others has." Lee played the devil's advocate.

"No," Powell said smugly. "Let me explain who can take *un*classified data from the computer, then see if you can guess what I've got in mind."

"Wait," Lee said. He got two beers from the refrigerator, gave one can to Powell, peeled the tab off his own. "Go ahead."

"Across the country," Doug said, "there are more than four hundred trunkline adjuncts to the main Defense Department computer. There's one in every university campus that's engaged in research for the military. And there's one in the research labs of every company involved in defense work. There's another on every military base from here to Alaska. Thousands of people—industry and college researchers, scientists, high-ranking military officers—must have access to reams of data that's kept on the unclassified mag drums in the computer's storage facilities. Every day, these people make thousands of data requests from the trunk line terminals all over the country. A programmer sits at one of these terminals and types out a request for information which is transmitted directly to the Pentagon main computer. The reply —the requested material—comes in the form of a long teletype sheet, a very neat printout. *Or* it comes on a transference line which records the data on a mag tape at the trunk line facility, so the researcher will have a permanent library and compact reference source that can be printed out at his leisure."

Lee looked past Powell, out the window.

Though it was only five o'clock, the day was nearly gone. The early winter night had crept in.

Lee watched random snowflakes strike the glass, and he smiled. The smile was not for the beauty of the snow, but for the beauty of Doug Powell's plan which he was just now beginning to grasp. "Somehow, you're going to use one of those trunk line terminals to obtain classified data. You could do it from somewhere here in New York. Or from California, as far as that goes."

"You're catching on."

His eyes refocused: from the snow to the man across the table. "But aren't these trunk lines guarded?"

"Only lightly. Night watchmen. Remember, unless you have the code words to open the top security data sections, the trunk-lines can't do you any good."

"But you have the code words."

"I sure do. And I have the binary numbers which represent the exact data addresses of important informational subtopics."

"You're losing me," Lee said.

"A data address is simply the specific coordinates in those fifteen thousand magnetic tape drums where any one subject is located."

"You got all this from your father?"

Powell nodded. He had made his third cigarette last until the very end, and now he nearly burned his fingers as he pressed out the short butt. "The old man received his new two-week code book the day before Christmas. When he carries it with him, there are guards. But when he's at home, he pops the book in the wall safe in the den. He was home all Christmas Day."

"And you know the safe's combination. You stole the book?"

Doug shook his head slowly. "No. If a book were missing, the computer would be locked and new codes would be immediately established. The book I stole would be worthless. I merely spent an hour looking through it, copying down those codes I thought most valuable. Then I put it back in the safe."

"So . . ."

"So, I go to one of these trunk lines. With your help, I overpower the guard or guards. I use the remote terminal to steal classified data from the Pentagon. I also steal the tapes containing the current overall program, because that's a key toward reading the other information we steal. Then we walk away, untouched."

It was incredible.

It was *terrifying.*

Lee knew that he should opt out now, refuse to listen to any more of this. But . . . Four million . . . Six million . . . "I have some questions," he said.

4.

"I've only given you a general summary of it," Powell said slowly. "The details of computer theory and practice would only bore you." For the first time in half an hour, he leaned back in his chair. "Otherwise, fire away."

"You know how to use one of these trunk line terminals?"

"The whole plan would be meaningless if I didn't. You know I've studied computer technology. A year and a half of it before I was drafted, and another year or so when I got out of the Army. That's one of the many things I decided wasn't for me—but I learned a hell of a lot. Enough for this job."

Lee got up and went to the sink. He turned on the cold water, washed his hands without soap, splashed his face. He dried on the dish towel. By the time he returned to the table, he was filmed with sweat again. "How will you deliver the ransom demand?"

"I'll use the trunk line terminal to teletype the demand right into the Pentagon."

It was madness.

But would it work?

"And if they're willing to pay, how do we pick up the money with the CIA and the FBI and everybody else lurking around the drop point?"

"I've got that figured," Doug said. "But that's another aspect of the job altogether. Let's hold on that until you've satisfied yourself with the rest of it."

"When this hits them, they're going to investigate those nine men who hold code books. And their families."

"I'll be able to account for myself." He wiped one big hand across his face, the first sign that he was weary from tension. It also seemed to indicate that he was relaxing now that he'd revealed the whole plan. "But they'll soon give up on those nine. They're sure to think it was done with some sophisticated electronic stuff. They'll see it as an international operation. The truth will be too simple to appeal to them."

"O.K.," Lee said. You raid the Pentagon computer. You get the data. The government's in a turmoil. They're willing to pay what you ask. But how will you *spend* it? It's going to be marked. There'll be an FBI agent in every bank in the country, waiting for the first marked bill to pass."

"We don't ask for money," Powell said. "The ransom will be something small and untraceable, something we can easily convert into cash, something that's worth about ten million and can be fenced for at least half its value."

"Like what?"

"It could be diamonds. But the CIA can cover the diamond market too easily. It could be heroin—but I find drug dealing distasteful."

"What does that leave?" Lee asked.

Powell told him, in detail. He had put a great deal of thought into it; now he was basking in Lee's appreciation of his cleverness.

"Something as small as that can be worth so much?" Lee asked.

"Easily."

He thought about it for several minutes. It was neat. Almost too neat. He felt as if there were some flaw in it that he was stupidly overlooking. "But then there's the fence to worry about."

"First of all, you must realize that while the fence will know we stole the merchandise, he won't realize that we held the entire future of the United States for ransom. The government is going to clamp a tight lid on its investigation. You'll never read about this in the newspapers, and neither will the fence. He won't have a chance to get cold feet. Furthermore, once a middleman's taken that ransom off our hands and given us cash for it, he's in it as deeply as we are. He'll be silent as a rock."

"You know someone who could fence it?"

"Remember Sergeant Dunio?" Powell smiled. "Well, he got into smuggling *objets d'art*, antiquities from the Northern Highlands, works that had been stolen from some of the temples . . . He met the right people, established a list of rich customers who have private collections. He's out of the Army, dealing full-time now. He even buys for some governments who don't mind furnishing their museums with pieces bought on the black market."

"The people he sells to—"

"Don't know his real name and couldn't trace either him or us. Anyway, I've talked to Dunio, and I think he'll take these five pieces, the ransom, to a government and not an individual. In this case, his customer is never going to aid the CIA's investigation."

It was looking better and better.

He searched desperately for a hole in it. "O.K. The government pays our ransom. We turn that over to Dunio. Dunio gives us a lot of unmarked cash . . . How do we explain our sudden wealth?"

"I've got my own plan, and it's private," Powell said. "However, I can make several suggestions for you. I'll put you in touch with a European lawyer, a man in Switzerland, a friend of Dunio's. This guy can establish a nonexistent relative for you, a mythical school chum, an old friend of your mother's—someone who was wealthy, died, and left you a quarter of a million. It'll be entirely fictitious, but it'll be damned thorough, with postdated records, death certificate, everything. Now, say this unexpected benefactor's bequest amounts to one or two hundred thousand after taxes. With that, you start a business to 'clean' the rest of your share of the money. You can even 'win' some of it in Las Vegas or Monaco."

Lee was impressed. "You've thought of everything."

Powell wasn't in the mood for modesty. "I have, yes."

"How do we pick up the ransom?"

"Simple." Powell grinned broadly. In the next five minutes, he outlined the plan for the payment of the ransom and the return of the mag tapes to the government.

It was damned good.

Hell, it was *perfect.*

Trembling, Lee finished his beer and tried to review every element of the scheme. It was science fiction. It was a dream that would dissolve into morning. Wasn't it?

Doug leaned forward. Like a glass under a water tap, he seemed to fill up again with nervous energy. "Admittedly, it's dangerous. But is it any more dangerous than the year we spent in Asia?"

"It's all so fast," Lee said. "It doesn't seem real."

"It's real enough," Powell said. "Look, this isn't just a chance for us to get rich quick. This isn't just a robbery—it's a goddamned social statement! All those gung-ho military men down there in D.C. smugly advocating brushfire engagements, policing actions, *war!* We'd be doing this country a favor if we upset their happy little world, showed them that in this mechanized age *any* nation is vulnerable. We'd strike deep into the heart of everything they hold sacred." He was speaking with passion now, with something like moral conviction. "And even when we gave the tapes back, after we had the ransom, they'd never forget what a blow was *almost* dealt them."

It was damned appealing.

"But when you wound a big animal," Lee said, "it comes at you with twice the rage it had before you hurt it." He fingered his scars. "It's come at me once. If it comes again . . ."

"You're getting philosophical," Powell said. "This is strictly a business deal." He laughed. "In fact, it's a peculiarly *American* business deal. We've got the profit motive."

Lee closed his eyes. "If I hang on a few more years, I'll be a full-fledged lawyer."

"And you'll be thirty-one, just starting. If you're lucky, you'll make your money just in time to retire. Face it, Lee. The war scooped years out of your life."

"Why risk it, Doug? You could have almost anything you want."

Frowning, Powell said, "My old man only gives something if he gets twice as much in return. And he controls Loretta. If I took anything from them, I'd always be in the general's grasp."

"I thought you got along well with them."

Powell grimaced. "My mother's the next thing to an alcoholic. The general . . . Look, didn't you ever wonder what the son of Norman Powell was doing in the war as an infantryman?"

Lee shrugged. "I thought you were proving you could handle yourself without your father's help."

Powell smiled, shook his head. "Christ, no! When I was drafted, I figured the general would take care of me. Instead, he made sure I was sent into the thick of it. He really believes it was good for me. Besides, it made him look pretty good in the eyes of the other boys down in D.C."

Lee wiped his face with one hand. "I don't know what to say, Doug. That's terrible. It's . . ."

Doug reached out and put one hand on Lee's left wrist, gripped him firmly. "We have the same motivations, you and me. We both want money. We both want to strike back."

"Strike deep . . ." Lee mused.

"Are you with me?"

"I don't know."

"You've got to decide soon. We've got to move within the next week or so, before those code words are outdated."

"There's so much to think about."

What was this? What was the matter with him? Why didn't he say no right now, this minute? How could he even consider this insane proposition?

"I'll have to know by nine tomorrow morning," Powell said. "I'm staying at the Algonquin. Room 34. I'm registered under the name Walters."

"If I start leaning your way," Lee said, "I'll want to hear the plan all over again, in detail."

"Sure." Powell got to his feet. The chair scraped noisily on the old linoleum. "You're going to come in with me. I know you. You've already accepted it. Now, you're just trying to justify it. And that won't take long."

"I'm not that close."

"Yes. You are." He stretched, throwing his long arms out to his side. "Nothing else? No more questions?"

"Not right now," Lee said.

Powell slipped into his coat, buttoned it. He looked like a stockbroker on his way home from a long day on the Street. "It'll be like old times, the two of us slugging it out against all of them.

With one important difference. This time around, we can win more than we can lose. And it's all for ourselves."

Together, they walked through the dark living room to the front door. "By nine in the morning," Doug said.

"Okay."

"Whether or not you want in."

"I'll call. I'll ask for Walters."

They did not shake hands.

Lee opened the door.

They exchanged one last look.

Douglas Powell went out into the hall and down the stairs and away.

Closing the door, Lee started to twist the safety lock. Then he realized that Carrie would be home soon, and he let the double latch alone.

"You can lock it," she said, behind him. "I've been home for some time now."

He whirled, surprised. "Carrie?"

She was standing in the kitchen archway, outlined by the low wattage lamp burning behind her. "You're going to do it, aren't you?"

He was too startled to reply.

"I came home forty minutes ago," she said. "I had my key. And you didn't have the safety lock on the door. I guess the radio covered the sounds I made coming in. I almost called out to you, but then I caught the drift of the conversation . . ."

He reached out and touched her face. "You've got to forget everything you heard, everything he said."

"Are you going to forget it?" she asked.

"Naturally. It was crazy."

"You won't forget, though. He was right about you. You're just trying to justify it now. You've already accepted it." She sighed. "And now we've got to figure out how I'll fit into it."

5.

The girl's name was Pia James. She was twenty-five, appeared to be younger but handled herself as if she were ten years more sophisticated. Halfway between five and six feet tall, she was willowy, with long, black hair and green eyes and a complexion like honey and milk blended in equal portions. She was wearing a long Paraphernalia sheath the color of oranges sprinkled with cinnamon, a three-hundred-dollar number with a high neck and a low hemline and a tendency to cling to her. She might have been a freshman or sophomore at Vassar, home for the holidays. Although the ripe outlines of her large, high breasts were exquisitely and almost obscenely detailed by the dress, she did not appear to be a whore. But she was.

An expensive whore.

Shortly past seven o'clock, she joined Douglas Powell at his table at the Spanish Pavilion. Three minutes after she sat down, she had one of the Pavilion's large drinks, a Jack Rose, clasped in both hands; she sipped at it with the timidity of a fawn testing the purity of spring water. Every move she made was graceful. She radiated an almost hypnotic tranquility. When they had been together for only a few minutes, Powell felt cut off from reality, as if he were afloat on a sea of color and noise which had no form. Pia James was the only solidity.

"I'm glad when you come to town," she said. She looked around at the clustered tables, the fine paintings, the high ceiling . . ."I know we'll be coming here."

He smiled ruefully. "You're glad to see me only because I take you to dinner at the Spanish Pavilion?"

"You know what I meant. You're one of the few men of mine who has any style, who's fun to be with."

"I'll bet you say that to all of them."

"Ahhh," she said, "you're in a masochistic mood."

He grinned. "And you're sadistic."

"I am whatever you want me to be," she said, smiling at him quite frankly.

He liked her self-assurance and the way it did not interfere at all with her femininity. She was quick, bright, and not particularly worried about losing a good customer. She knew that she could always find others.

He understood her, because he had become familiar with prostitutes. Since he had come back from the war, he had been to bed with nearly two dozen of them. He had no steady girl friend. He had no girl friend at all. When he considered the time and energy necessary to carry on a courtship, he did not want a close relationship with a woman. Besides, for some reason he could not explain, he was far more aroused by a woman if he was paying for her.

He was paying for Pia James.

And from the moment she had entered the restaurant and started toward his corner table, he had wanted her very badly.

They spent more than two hours with drinks, the excellent *solomillo al chef*, a pitcher of sweetened sangria, and pine nut cake. When they were having coffee and brandy, he said, "How would you like to make five thousand dollars for two hours of work?"

Her head was slightly lowered as she stirred her coffee. She looked up at him through long dark lashes. "It sounds too arduous."

"It has nothing to do with your profession," he said quietly. "I need someone to run an errand for me. In a week or so. A very special errand."

She said nothing. She merely watched him, waiting to hear the rest of it.

"You would have to board a certain subway train at a certain hour; locate a man who has a package for me. You pick it up and take it off the train and bring it to me."

"Why don't you pick it up yourself?" She had lowered her already soft voice.

"It's nothing illegal," he said. "It's just that he and I work for opposite business interests. And he may have a private detective on his tail. We wouldn't want to be seen together."

"What's in this box?" she asked.

"You needn't know. And you don't have to tell me right now whether or not you're interested. Just think about it. And try to think of another girl you could use to help you."

She was perplexed. "Why would I need help? It sounds easy."

"It's more complex than I've said," he admitted. "I've only given you the general outline, so you can think about it. Roll it around in your head for a while. If you're interested, we can talk about it later."

Her pretty lips drew into a bow, and her eyelids came down until she was looking at him through heavy lashes. "Five thousand?"

He nodded.

"Two hours work?"

"Maybe less."

"I'll think about it."

He knew, then, that she would do it. He had his double-blind, one of the two messengers he would need for the ransom pickup.

An hour later, when he came out of the bathroom at the hotel, she had turned down the bedclothes. She said, "It's chilly in here. I've put the thermostat up all the way."

He slid his arms around her from behind. "Let me put *your* thermostat up all the way."

She laughed, leaned back against him.

"Let me—" he began.

"We don't need any more talk," she said. She pushed her buttocks up and back, grinding against him.

He unbuttoned her dress, pulled it down over her slim shoulders.

Lowering her arms, she let the sheath slide away. An instant later she was standing in a puddle of soft orange cloth.

Reaching from behind her, he caressed her breasts and gently thumbed her erect nipples until she shivered and turned and embraced him. He kissed her eyes, then spent long minutes with her warm mouth. He allowed her to undress him, and he finished undressing her.

On the bed, twenty minutes later, he said, "Now." Poised over her, his knees between her opened thighs and his thin but muscular arms supporting him, he looked down at her Vassar face, focused on her beautiful green eyes. "Tell me."

Knowing precisely what was expected, as did all the girls he patronized, she said, "Your father's dead." She raised her hips, helped him enter her. "Your mother's dead." Her voice was a whisper, yet sharp as a blade. She alternated between the two sentences, announcing first one fantasized death and then the other, over and over, until the words lost their true meaning and assumed a mesmeric meaning all of their own.

He was strange, she thought. And she supposed he was very sick. Down inside, he might even be an ugly and violent man. But he had never hurt her. Therefore, strange as it was, disgusting as it was, she did not mind at all. While he moved in and out of her, she told him his parents were dead. Other men had asked her to do worse things. By comparison, this was easy money.

He closed his eyes. His movements became more and more furious.

When they had both dressed and he had given her an envelope which contained two hundred dollars in twenties, she said, "About that five-thousand-dollar errand. I certainly am interested."

He sat on the edge of the bed. "I knew you would be."

"You want to tell me exactly what I have to do?" She was standing by the television set, and she switched it on, turning up the volume to cover their voices. No one in the adjoining rooms would be able to hear them. She was acting surprisingly like a pro, like someone who was accustomed to taking part in shady conspiracies to circumvent if not break the law. "And why do I need another girl?"

He told her only what she had to know, and he filled in the rest with lies.

"When do I get paid?"

"Twenty-five hundred before the job. Twenty-five hundred after it's finished and I have the box. You pay the other girl out of yours. She shouldn't want more than a hundred or two."

She stood in front of the television set, bracketed by slim lines of colored light from the left and right edges of the tube, and she began to nervously tap one foot. "What's in the box?"

"I told you, you don't have to know."

"What if it's horse?"

"Heroin?" He grimaced. "Pia, I've explained. It's nothing like that. It's industrial espionage. You'll get the box from a man who has raided his company's research division. He's passing over memos and files on their forthcoming products." He went through the whole phony story one more time.

"You're not telling me the truth," she said.

He sighed, shrugged. "Maybe you don't want to know it."

She stood there for a full minute, tapping her foot, staring over his head at the far wall. "Well, even if it *is* uncut skag, and even if the cops do nail me with it, I can plead ignorance. There'll be some bad moments . . . But I'll come through."

"It isn't drugs," he insisted.

"Five thousand . . ."

"That's right."

"O.K.," she said, suddenly determined. "You have an errand girl."

"I'll call you in about a week to set the time and place," he told her as he helped her on with her coat.

When she closed the door behind her, when he was alone, he started to laugh. Everything was falling into place. He was going to make it work!

He was in high spirits and drinking Scotch when the telephone rang at a quarter past one in the morning. He fumbled for it, sat up in bed. "Hello?"

"Mr. Walters?"

He recognized the voice at once. Lee Ackridge. "Yes?"

"I've been giving a lot of thought to that computer deal we discussed."

"So have I," Powell said, knowing what was coming. As he spoke, he put down his Scotch glass on the bedside table. Holding the receiver in his left hand, he picked up the Scotch bottle and poured himself another round. He would use it to celebrate.

"I'm sorry to call you this late," Lee said. "But I knew I couldn't get to sleep until I'd committed myself. I'm definitely interested. Can you come over here in the morning? We need to iron out some fine wrinkles."

"Ten o'clock?" Powell asked.

"That would be good."

"See you in the morning, then."

"One more thing," Ackridge said.

There was something in Lee's voice that took the smile off Powell's face. "What is it?"

"My partner came back while you were here and heard most of your proposition."

"Your partner?"

"The lady who's here with me," Lee said. "Anyway, she wants in on the deal."

"Impossible. This is man's business," Powell said, realizing he was only conducting a holding action.

"I tend to agree with you," Lee said. He sounded as if he were in a much better mood than he had been this afternoon. "But I'm labeled a male chauvinist when I say that. So . . . It looks like my partner's going to have to be involved. If there's no place for her, I'll have to bow out."

"You mean that?"

"I guess I do."

Powell made a face, shook his head slowly back and forth, then realized Ackridge could not see him. "Christ, I don't know anything about her. Is she sensible? Trustworthy?"

"Do you remember," Lee asked, "when we were discussing the middleman? Our friend Mr. Dunio? You said that once he was involved, he could be trusted to protect his own interests and, therefore, ours too. Well, the same thing ought to apply to my partner. Once she's involved, you can count on her."

"*Damn!*" Powell said.

"If you're worried about the profit split," Lee said, "it'll be the same as you proposed. Fifty-fifty. She'll share in my half."

"That's not it. A *woman.*" Since the war, he had come to think of women as disposable merchandise.

"If it doesn't appeal to you," Lee said, "we can cancel the whole idea. You'll be free to go elsewhere. It'll be as if you never discussed it with me."

Powell hesitated. Then: "No. It's a three-way deal."

"Fine," Lee said. "I'll see you at ten tomorrow."

"At ten," Powell said. He hung up.

After he had talked to Ackridge, Doug Powell was no longer in high spirits. Everything had been falling neatly into place, just as he had envisioned it, and then . . . A woman! A change of plans, because of a woman. For God's sake, didn't Lee understand how serious this was? How could he *not* understand? If they made one mistake, they could get their asses busted.

For a moment, he had been tempted to tell Lee to forget it, drop the bastard and find someone else. But that was impossible. He would need another couple of weeks to find a replacement, and a month or two more to check out the new man. Even then, he would not be able to rely on anyone else as thoroughly as he could on Lee.

Christ.

A woman!

He watched television without seeing it.

He drank too much Scotch.

Finally—whether he was uplifted by the liquor, or whether he went through one of the sudden mood changes which had plagued him recently—he began to feel better. O.K. So there was a woman in on it now, a third party whom he had not expected. It wasn't getting out of hand. Not at all. Lee was still there. Lee would not have suggested bringing her in with them unless he could control her. Lee would handle her. It would be cool. Just fine.

And there was a decided benefit arising out of this. Now, Powell did not feel the least bit guilty about lying to Lee.

Ackridge believed they would never turn the mag tapes over to an agent of another country. But Powell had already made contacts. Whether or not the ransom was paid, those mag tapes full of top secret data would be passed on to a foreign agent.

Considering all they had gone through together and had been to each other, Powell had felt ashamed of lying to Lee. Of course, the lie had been necessary. He had known that Ackridge was ripe for a caper that would make him rich, but he had also known that Lee would never go the whole route and sell the country down the river. Lee had nothing to gain by that, as Powell did . . . But now that Ackridge had rung in this girl, had pulled this third-party crap, Powell felt better. If he were not being exactly fair to his old buddy, it was also true that his old buddy had not been fair to him.

Wasn't it? Wasn't it true?

He undressed and switched off the television set, turned out the lights. Dizzy from Scotch, he lay down in the center of the bed where he could still smell Pia James's perfume.

The room spun around.

Your father is dead.

Your mother is dead.

"Oh, no," he told the darkness. "They're not dead. It's much better than that."

They would still be alive when this was finished, but they would wish they were dead. They would lose everything they loved: acceptance in the best Washington social circles, public respect, dignity, an opportunity to amass really huge wealth and power . . . Once his contact had those tapes, the United States would lose everything, but more important than that, the general and sweet Loretta would also lose everything. After all, they would be the parents of the villain of the century. He would admit the theft of the data and take the responsibility for the ruination of his country. And that would be the end of the general.

Smiling at the lightless room, he slept.

6.

Paul Freneau did not think of himself as a criminal.

Outwardly, he appeared to be an honest, hard-working, hard-living, fortunate young man. At thirty-two he was beginning his eighth year as an interpreter at the United Nations; with a French father and a Spanish mother who had immigrated to the United States in the late thirties, he had been a natural for his job. He did well enough to keep a pleasant apartment in Manhattan. He drove a good car, dressed well, and was seen with beautiful but obviously "nice" girls. Every other year, he managed a full month's vacation in Europe.

However, he had found that he could not possibly maintain his desired life-style on the salary of an interpreter. After all, his apartment was on one of the best blocks of East Sixty-fourth Street. His car was a Mark IV, his clothes from Bill Blass, his girl friends from the better families. When he went to Europe, he went first class, and there was no hotel or restaurant he would deny himself merely because of its prices.

He had discovered, near the end of his first year at the United Nations, that he could handsomely supplement his salary by performing favors for delegates and second-level ambassadors who were assigned to the world organization. Mostly, he delivered messages. Usually, these were between one and another of those foreign dignitaries, between two men who wished to hold private discussions on a subject over which, in public, they appeared to be bitterly and irreconcilably divided. Occasionally, there were American citizens—wheeler-dealers, businessmen, politicians—who wished to pass something on to a UN delegate without personally phoning or meeting him. These people called Freneau. And Freneau forwarded their messages. It was quite easy, and it earned him far more money than he received for his daily toil in the translator's booth.

When he had first begun passing along these inquiries, requests, warnings, bits of advice, and even coded messages, Freneau had worried about his safety. He *knew* he was acting only as an amateur diplomat and not as a funnel for espionage. But how would others view it? What would, say, the FBI think?

Most of the contacts he made were with representatives of nations which could in no way be construed as enemies of the United States. England. France. Italy. Sweden, Spain, Japan, Greece . . .

Eventually, as astonishingly substantial sums rolled in as payment for his services, Freneau realized that any thorough FBI investigation would surely exonerate him of any false charges of espionage or even improper conduct. He was merely one of those very necessary amateurs who oiled the works of international diplomacy.

His conscience stopped bothering him. He stopped worrying about his safety. He slept well.

At six o'clock on the morning of December 27, the telephone woke him from one of those sound sleeps.

He picked up the receiver. "Paul Freneau."

The voice at the far end of the line was low and cold. "Are you acquainted with Mr. Zaitsev?"

"Ilya? Of course."

"When you see him today, would you please tell him that Dan Walters called you?"

Freneau used one thin hand to push his hair out of his eyes. He suppressed a yawn. "Certainly. Is that all I'm to tell him? Just that you called?"

"One other thing," Walters said. "Tell him that I've got my team together."

"You've got your team together?" Freneau asked. It was not that he was confused. He was accustomed to passing along messages which made little or no sense to him but which were meaningful to those for whom they had been intended. He repeated what Walters had said only to be sure that he had heard him correctly and could deliver the line properly to Zaitsev.

"You've got it right," Walters said. "Thank you."

"Excuse me," Freneau said quickly, before the stranger could hang up.

"Yes."

"I hate to sound cross . . . But if you need me in the future, would you not call so early? I usually don't get up until seven thirty, you see."

"Sure," Walters said.

The line clicked, went dead.

That was Paul Freneau's first contact with Powell-Walters. It was also his last. He was, after all, only one drop of oil in the intricate works of international diplomacy.

Like Paul Freneau, Roy Genelli woke at six o'clock.

He had not been roused by a telephone or even by an alarm. He automatically woke at six, every morning of the week. It was habit.

During his first five years with the Bureau, when Genelli had been a rookie field agent, there had been no routine in his life, no system, no sense of order. He was always on a stakeout or tailing a suspect or running down a lead, moving, chasing, or waiting to move and chase, studying the prey . . . There had been nights when he went without sleep. And even when the workload had not been so heavy as to demand that sort of sacrifice, his bedtime had varied wildly from one night to the next. Fifteen years ago, when he had gotten some seniority and a couple of promotions, he was able to enjoy a more traditional workday. He had begun to go to bed at ten o'clock in the evening, because it was such a luxury to be between the sheets at that hour. It had become a habit, as had the six o'clock rising time. Now that he was a special assistant to the supervisor of the Middle-Eastern District and could pretty much set his own schedule, there was little chance that anything could spoil his comfortable routine.

As he would have done on a working day, Genelli got out of bed at once. He stepped into his slippers and pulled on a tattered bathrobe which he belted at the waist.

He had worked over the long holiday weekend in order to free other men who had families. Now, he was spending three days at home. He always worked the holidays. For one thing, they were easy, quiet. Few arrests were made, and hardly any new cases came up on a holiday. Besides, putting in a full nine or ten hours at the office made Christmas Day less lonely than it would have been otherwise.

At forty-two, Roy Genelli had never been married. He certainly was not a woman hater, nor was he even awkward around women. At five-ten and a hundred and eighty pounds, he was a bit overweight but not fat. He usually wore a brown suit that blended with his brown hair and brown eyes, making him look plain; yet he was not unattractive. There was always someone whom he was dating—and sometimes bedding. But thus far he had never hooked into anything that he had wanted to last. Although it was, at times, lonely, he did not dislike his bachelorhood. It was a way to live.

He picked up his glasses from the nightstand, put them on, and blinked away the sleep matter at the corners of his eyes.

Just then, the alarm clock rang.

Although he had not failed to wake within five minutes of six any day within the last decade, Genelli always set his alarm. To do so was not merely habit, but one facet of his thoroughness. Roy Genelli was an extremely thorough man. He rarely forgot or overlooked anything.

He went downstairs and cooked breakfast, ate at the table by the large window in the dining room.

His narrow town house was on a quiet block of G Street, flanked by other town houses, shielded from the street by two old elm trees which had somehow survived the blight for several generations. It was no palace, but it was a comfortable place to be. Lately, he had come to see it more and more as a haven.

He ate, looked at the elm trees, and thought about how sour his work at the Bureau had become for him. Twenty years ago, it had been exciting. And he had felt as if he were accomplishing something. But these days . . . You worked yourself sick establishing an airtight case against some hood who imported heroin from Montreal, you nailed him down tight, and you got him sent up for twenty years. But what did it really matter? A week after you arrested him, another hood had stepped in and taken over the Montreal connections. As long as the addicts were not given either straight H or methadone by the government, they'd buy it through the underworld. You could never take a step ahead without sliding one step back. And if you weren't chasing the drug kings, you were trying to build a case against an interstate pornographic film dealer. Or you were prying into the mundane activities of suspect political groups . . . These days, it was all sour, because no one cared to solve the *real* crimes; how easy, instead, to worry about the crimes that had no victims.

He finished his breakfast, took the dirty dishes out to the kitchen and washed them.

When a man had no family, Genelli thought, he should have a career to which he could give himself. But what if, after twenty years of giving, he discovered that the career was not worthy of him? What if he admitted he was wasting his life? At forty-two, having been nothing but a cop, was a man too old to start out in a new field?

As he dried the silverware, he wondered how long it had been since he'd worked on a case that he found worthwhile. Five years? No. God, it was even longer than that. Eight years? Nine? Ten? Keep going. Eleven? Twelve? With something of a shock, he realized that it had been fourteen years since the Zilinski-Ross killing spree . . . That bloody case, with its twelve murders and eighteen robberies, had propelled him through twenty-six states in a harrowing investigation and chase which had taxed his ingenuity and intelligence. And without a doubt, that had been his last challenging assignment.

Fourteen years!

God knew, he didn't wish any more Zilinski-Ross horrors on innocent people. But there should be something . . . If he had to send men skulking around after one more pornographer, he'd feel like coming home and blowing his brains out.

No. He wouldn't let it get him down that far. He would retire before then. Hell, he had twenty years in now. He could quit today—or hold out for twenty-five and a higher pension. It was a difficult truth to deal with, but Roy Genelli had to admit that he would probably never again have a chance to apply himself to interesting, worthwhile investigative work.

Pouring a second cup of coffee, he started to think more seriously about the various careers a forty-two-year-old cop might reasonably hope to begin.

NEW YEAR'S EVE

The Theft

7.

On the afternoon of December 31, Lee and Carrie caught a train to Philadelphia, where they met Doug Powell by the terminal's Thirtieth Street entrance, just as planned.

Powell took their single suitcase out of Lee's hand and preceded them through the station doors. "I've rented a car," he said.

They found it too cold to pause and talk. The sky was bright blue, but a stiff wind raced along the street. Carrie huddled against Lee, and the two of them followed Powell to a year-old Chevrolet Impala.

Powell put the suitcase in the back. The three of them rode up front. Carrie sat between the two men, while Powell drove.

Looking at the gray buildings rising up on all sides, Lee said, "I guess it's no different from New York. But I've always hated Philadelphia."

"In a week," Powell said, "when you're rolling in money, you'll have a soft spot in your heart for Philly."

"I doubt it," Lee said. "Where are we going now?"

"The hotel," Powell said. He accelerated through a changing light, slowed down again.

Sitting beside the tall man, wrapped up tightly in her furry coat, Carrie appeared to be much smaller and more fragile than she really was. "Something just occurred to me which *should* have occurred to me before this."

Powell looked sideways at her. He had not yet gotten used to her, to the idea that she would participate.

"What's that?" Lee asked.

She squinted against the sun's glare on the windshield. "What if someone spots the car tonight? I know there's almost no chance of it. But what if someone sees it at the university and tells the cops about it tomorrow?"

"That won't matter," Powell said. "The name and address on the Hertz records isn't mine. The car is leased to Daniel Walters."

"How'd you manage that?" Lee asked.

Powell smiled, pleased with himself. "I have a full set of papers in the Walters name." He wheeled the car right, swung it around a city bus. "Social Security card, driver's license from the state of Virginia, birth certificate, even a passport."

Carrie looked at Lee and frowned.

Lee said, "Where in the hell did you get all of that?"

"Dunio."

"You know him better than you did when we were together."

"Remember," Powell said, "I was there a few months after you were shipped home to a hospital. In wartime, you can get to know a man pretty damned fast. And Dunio's an easy man to get to know, war or no war."

Lee shook his head wonderingly. "And on top of everything

else that he's doing, Dunio's a forgery artist?"

"Not him. But he knows one. Hell, he must know a dozen of them by now, one in every city where he has customers: New York, San Francisco, Tokyo, Singapore, Hong Kong, Paris, London . . ." He stopped for a red light, looked at Lee. "I did some jobs for Dunio in Asia, after you were sent home and our company got moved back to Saigon. We got to know and like each other. Before I was shipped out, I asked him to help me get a set of papers."

"And he did."

"He sure did," Powell said, smiling.

"But why did you want them?"

Powell shrugged. "Seemed like a good thing to have. Still does. I get the driver's license updated every year, keep the papers in shape."

"But surely," Carrie said, "you weren't planning anything criminal three years ago?"

"Well, it must have been in the back of my mind." Powell smiled.

The light turned green.

The Impala surged ahead.

On the twenty-seventh of December and again on the twenty-eighth, Douglas Powell had called the Sheraton Hotel in downtown Philadelphia to reserve a room, one room each time. On the first call, he booked a double overnight accommodation for Mr. and Mrs. Daniel Walters. On the twenty-eighth, he reserved a room for himself, using his real name.

Now, at four o'clock in the afternoon of the last day of the year, Lee and Carrie checked in, using Powell's false papers, and were shown to a clean and comfortable room on the tenth floor. Powell would check in fifteen minutes later. He had told them he would use another phony name; but that was not the case at all. It never occurred to either of them that Powell would *want* to leave a trail.

When the bellboy had gone, Carrie went to the room's only window, pulled back the drapes, and stared out at the city.

Lee watched her. She was wearing a long black skirt and a blue poorboy sweater which matched the color of her eyes, and she looked wonderful. For the first time in weeks, he felt a stirring in his groin. If there were time, he was fairly sure he could make love to her. But Doug would be calling soon; in minutes the three of them would be meeting here to discuss the plan one last time.

From her place by the window, she said, "Lee, do you think there's something odd about him?"

"Doug?"

"Yes."

"How do you mean?"

"I don't know . . ."

He got out of the chair beside the telephone and went to the window, stood beside her. "He's just nervous."

"It's more than nervousness," she insisted.

"He hasn't changed in four days."

"I know. I thought he was acting strange when he was at the apartment, in New York. He doesn't seem to be able to look either you or me in the eye. And his moods go up and down too fast. Watch his face. One moment he's smiling. The next, he looks like he might cry. He—"

"It's only the pressure."

"Just the same," she said, "keep an eye on him."

He put one hand on her shoulder. "You want to back out of this?"

"No."

"We still can."

"No," she said. "Just keep an eye on him."

8.

Sitting in the front seat of the Chevy, Carrie tried not to think of all the things that might go wrong. She stared at the dark road ahead and at the oncoming headlights of other cars, and she listened to Doug Powell who had been babbling on the edge of senselessness ever since they had left the hotel.

Right now, he was telling them about tonight's target . . .

Founded in 1848 on a grant of one thousand acres of federal land, Langhorn University was an oasis of peace and beauty in the desert of suburban sprawl. Spotted with groves of elms and oaks, sycamores, birch trees and willows, the campus lay ten miles north of Philadelphia, twenty-six buildings which accommodated nine thousand students with plenty of room to spare.

As he drove the rented Impala north, farther out of the city, Powell chattered on about the history and ambience of Langhorn.

He spoke so rapidly that his words sometimes ran together and were difficult to understand.

Carrie listened to him and occasionally looked to see what his face might reveal. So far as she could tell, none of this information about Langhorn affected their plan or their chances for successfully executing the theft. It was just filler. Babbling. Powell was talking chiefly to prevent her and Lee from expressing or being overwhelmed by last-minute doubts. The longer she was around Powell, the more easily she could see through him. However, she could not yet penetrate that central mystery, the thing about him that made the chills run down her back.

Since 1964, Powell explained, Langhorn had been one of the world's leading centers for the study of computer design and theory. With another federal grant nearly as generous as that first gift of land, the Recard Institute for Computer Science had been built in the northwest corner of the campus. A considerable portion of the funds for the construction, furnishing, and budgeting of the Institute had come from the Defense Department. Computers were fast becoming—if not the generals of the future, then—the advisors to the generals of the future. The Defense Department wanted to be sure its transistorized strategists were as advanced as those being built in China and Russia. It was spending freely in order to maintain computer parity with enemy systems. Naturally, vast sums of money tempted many academics. Over the last two decades, even before the Recard Institute was built, as if in reaction to the increasingly anti-military attitudes of other educators, more than a hundred of Langhorn's faculty had become involved in Pentagon planning and weapons development.

Carrie saw that Powell's mouth was turned down, grim. He was staring ahead, eyes bright, as if he saw something more exciting than the highway.

It was to Langhorn, Powell explained for the fourth time, that he had come to study computer engineering in the early months after he'd gotten home from Asia. Now, for tonight's robbery, he had chosen this terminal of the Defense Department's data network because he knew it so well. If there were a remote chance that he might be seen and recognized after having been away for two years, that danger was easily balanced by the advantage of familiarity.

As Doug jabbered away, Carrie looked at Lee, caught his attention, made a face to express her concern over Powell's behavior.

Lee smiled. He leaned over and kissed her cheek.

She knew that he still thought Doug was only nervous. But it was clearly more than that. What? Was Powell's problem strictly private? Or was it something that would have broader consequences, something that would affect them? *Destroy* them?

At ten-thirty New Year's Eve, Powell turned the Impala into Ox Lane, the residential street which flanked the northwest perimeter of the campus and passed in front of the Recard Institute. The university lay on their left, rising up and back on low hills, fading into trees and shadows and finally into intense darkness. On the right was a series of old, stately stone houses. That was all as it should be, just as Doug had described it. Unexpectedly, however, Ox Lane was lined on both sides with parked cars, far more of them than could possibly belong to the people who lived here.

"What's this all about?" Lee asked.

Carrie saw it at once. Disconcerted, she pointed to a building at the far end of the first block, a three-story Victorian house on a large corner lot. All the lights were blazing. The front door stood open despite the chilly night air. A fan of amber light spread out from the door and glowed softly on the thinly snow-covered lawn.

"A New Year's Eve party," Lee said. He turned to Powell, who had slowed the car to a crawl. "You think this changes anything?"

"Well . . . I should have expected it." He stopped the car

altogether, in the middle of the street. "Most of these old houses are owned by Langhorn professors, deans, and administrators. At least one of them was bound to throw a big party tonight." He watched a young couple climb out of one of the parked cars and walk down to the house on the corner. "But it's no problem for us," he said, finally.

He was probably right, Carrie thought. But she also had the feeling that he would not give up the plan even if it became evident that they had no chance at all. If they had found the Institute ringed with uniformed policemen, Powell would still have wanted to go through with the robbery.

"I agree," Lee said. "The party gives us cover. Nobody's going to look out a window and wonder what we're doing here. We'll seem like just another bunch on our way to the house on the corner."

"Where's the Institute?" Carrie asked.

Powell indicated a four-story brick building with long, rectangular windows. "There."

Recard Institute was set a hundred feet back from the street, directly across Ox Lane from the house where the revelers were awaiting midnight.

"I don't like it," she said.

"You don't have to like it," Powell replied sharply. "You just sit here in the car and let us take care of everything."

She was about to snap back at him when Lee took her hand and squeezed it. "We'll be okay. We've been through worse than this, God knows. We can take care of ourselves."

As if he regretted the way he had spoken to her, Powell said, "Look, they're all drunk anyway. Right? What other reason is there for going to a New Year's Eve party? Everyone gets drunk. Even if they saw us, they wouldn't remember us later. They're inside the house, not outside. They're not watching us. They're impressing each other, seducing each other . . ."

Carrie sighed resignedly. "Let's hurry. Let's get it over and done with."

"I'm for that," Lee said.

Doug found a place to park on the right-hand side of the street, two hundred feet down from the corner house, across the street from the campus. He backed the Chevy in to the curb, positioning it between a Volkswagen and a Thunderbird. He straightened the wheel, dimmed the lights, but kept the engine running.

A ghostly luminescence from the widely separated streetlamps haunted the interior of the Chevy. It was not even bright enough to fully define their faces. Anyone outside would have to approach to within a few feet of the car to see that anyone was in it.

"Got the tools?" Powell asked.

Lee picked up a small black satchel from the floor between his feet. He put it on his lap, opened it. He took out two revolvers, both Colt Diamondbacks, .38 Specials. Passing one of them over to Powell, he kept the other gun for himself.

Carrie had seen the revolvers earlier, when Doug had come to their hotel room. But now, in the darkness, with the pale light barely glinting on their hard black lines, the weapons looked much more deadly than they had before. She began to wonder if she had made a fatal mistake in convincing Lee that he really wanted to join Powell in the robbery and that it was really the best thing for him to do.

Powell saw she was frightened. "Don't worry," he said, with uncharacteristic tenderness. "We don't have to use them."

"Then why take them?" she asked.

"No night watchman is going to back down from us just because we threaten him with our fists," Powell said. "But the sight of a couple of guns will stop him from doing anything foolish."

Lee took a box of ammunition from the satchel. He and Powell loaded the Colts.

"Time to move," Powell said. He tucked the gun in his coat

pocket and got out of the car, slamming the door behind himself.

Lee hesitated a moment, leaned close to Carrie. "I know how you feel. You're wondering what we've gotten into."

She bit her lip, nodded.

"Don't worry about it. You were right when you said we couldn't walk away from this."

She kissed him. "I wish I could go in with you."

"The two of us can be quicker, quieter, and cleaner about it," he said. "We're just applying military training to a civilian situation. You'll have a part in it later."

"Go on, then," she said. "Don't keep him waiting. Get it done with, and get back to me."

He initiated the kiss this time. Then, smiling crookedly, he opened his door and climbed out of the car, taking the gun and the satchel of tools with him.

Cold winter wind rushed over her.

Because both of Lee's hands were full, she pulled the door shut for him. The car's dim ceiling light winked out; the wan beams of the streetlamps returned. She was alone.

Sliding over behind the steering wheel, she watched them as they met in the middle of the street and walked across to the Langhorn campus. They did not hurry. They did not want to appear to be at all secretive. She was most likely the only one who was watching them, but they could not count on being unobserved. Both men were wearing jeans, short but heavy winter coats, long scarves wound around their necks . . . They could easily pass for university students who, for some reason, had returned early from the holiday recess.

In a moment they had gained the far sidewalk, and beyond that the snow-filmed grass. The shadows took hold of them, folded black fingers, and pulled them out of sight.

They had entered the campus almost a hundred yards from the Recard Institute, and now they would be circling around to approach the opposite face of the building from that which fronted on Ox Lane. Three lamp posts marked the walkway which wound toward the computer center. She hoped to catch sight of Lee as he passed those lights. But they were too good, trained to be stealthy. She saw nothing more of them.

She looked south along Ox Lane. No traffic.

She used the driver's side mirror to look north, back the way they had come. No traffic in that direction, either. Just dark, deserted pavement.

Her long wait had begun.

Her thoughts drifted inexorably back to the twenty-sixth, the day after Christmas, to the strange conversation between Lee and Powell which she had accidentally overheard . . .

She had been shocked when, quite early in that fantastic exchange between the two men, it had become clear that Lee was giving the proposition serious consideration. However, even more shocking was the realization, only minutes later, that she, too, was beginning to find the plan attractive. Standing against the wall in the lightless living room, only inches away from the kitchen arch, she had felt like a naughty little girl snooping on adults—and then suddenly she had been charged with a distinctly adult excitement at the notion of committing the crime which Doug Powell so meticulously outlined.

For hours after Powell had gone, they discussed it. They were both surprised to discover they were capable of participating in a conspiracy and crime of this magnitude.

Now, days later, she was still wondering about that when the passenger door opened, and someone said, "Hey! Hello there!"

She looked up, surprised, as the cold air struck her.

A thin, sandy-haired man in his late thirties was leaning in the open door, smiling drunkenly at her. His eyes were blue and blood-shot, his hair in complete disarray. He was wearing a suit but had loosened his tie and shirt collar. He resembled Red

Buttons. "Hey, what you doin' out here?" he asked, pushing the door open wider and leaning in even farther. "Should be inside. That's where the action is!"

She looked across the street at the dark campus, then back at the intruder. She had to get rid of him. How? She said, "You mean inside, at the party?"

"Where else?"

"I thought it was boring," Carrie said.

He blinked several times, as if she had spoken in a foreign tongue. "Boring?"

"Yes," she said. "You must think so too. Otherwise, why are you out here?"

"Got too hot in there," he said, waving again at the house. "Got like a damned furnace in there. Had to come out and cool off." His face, which had gone slack with incomprehension, now gathered up in a sly smile. He made a show of peeking into the back seat. "Out here with someone? Out here necking?" he asked.

He was drunk, next thing to falling-down-drunk. He would not require much encouragement to stay and chat. Silence was probably the best way to get rid of him; therefore, she said nothing.

"Now," he said, thickly, "I've offended you." His face seemed to slide apart into dozens of vertical lines. "I'm sorry. I didn't mean anythin' by it."

She stared straight ahead at the trunk of the Thunderbird parked in front of the Chevy.

"I swear I wasn't makin' a pass," he said. Abruptly, he slid into the car and sat down, pulled the door shut.

"Hold on just a minute," Carrie said, abandoning the tactic of silence.

"Wait now! Wait now!" he said, holding up his flattened hands as if to ward off blows. "I can't go away and let you think badly of me. Can I? Can't let you think I came out here and made a crude, an ugly pass at you. I got a reputation." He burped. "I want to take a minute and explain."

"You don't have to explain—"

"Ho there!" he said, holding up his hands again. He slipped a few inches farther down in the seat. "At least, give me a chance." He dropped his hands into his lap, then brought them up and massaged his temples as if he were searching with his fingertips for deeply imbedded splinters. "Besides . . . I don't think I can get up again."

"Look here—"

"I really *can't*," he insisted. "Not for a few minutes. I'm awfully damned dizzy. Got to take a couple of minutes to settle my old head."

He was not going to make a pass. He was too drunk and more than likely too meek to pose any physical threat.

Nevertheless, she had to get rid of him before Lee and Doug returned with the tapes. She was still wearing her long skirt and sweater; and with a coat covering most of that, she could probably pass as a refugee from the party. But Lee and Doug were wearing jeans, work shirts, and casual coats. Even to this drunk, they would not look like a part of the well-dressed crowd at the party.

"You aren't mad at me, are you?" he asked.

"No."

"Good! I'm glad." He stopped massaging his head, laced his fingers and cracked his knuckles. "My name's Wilbur Harttle," he said. "What's yours?"

She hesitated.

"I promise I'm makin' no pass," Harttle said. "Come on. What's your name?"

"Grace Kelly."

"Just like the old movie star?" he asked. "How about that!"

"Yeah," Carrie said. "How about that." She saw that she was not going to get rid of him easily, and she struggled against panic.

9.

Sweeping the land like a witch's broom, the wind rattled the bare branches of the trees. It was, Lee thought, like Halloween night.

The two of them lay in the grass, heedless of the half-inch of snow that melted under them. They were in an area of fairly deep darkness, although the campus sloping up behind them was even blacker. They could not be silhouetted for any watchman who might glance out of a window at the Recard Institute.

From their current perspective, the east side or campus-facing wall of the computer building resembled the ramparts of a heavily defended fortress. But that was an emotional view, Lee thought. There *were* ways to get inside. Not through any of the four glass doors at the main entrance, of course. Those would be locked. And they were too well lighted. He and Doug would have to go for one of the long, rectangular windows on the ground floor. Most of these were lightless, the rooms behind them untenanted.

"See anyone?" Powell asked.

"Faces at windows, you mean?"

"Yeah."

"Nothing."

"Me either."

The branches rattled like dangling skeletons.

"Why'd you ask?" Lee wanted to know. "You think maybe the watchman knows we're coming?" In Vietnam, they had always indulged in pessimistic, even gruesome jokes. It was a way to relieve the tension, to keep from getting so tightly wound up that you couldn't think straight. "He's probably in there with a primed cannon, ready to blow our heads off."

"Never can tell," Powell said rather sharply. He was in no mood for jokes.

Lying there, shivering as the snow soaked into his clothes, Lee gradually grasped the important difference between this operation and the risks they had taken in the war. Overseas, the danger had been greater. However, in the war they had been acting under orders. Here, no one was on their side. They were up against everyone and everything—except each other.

"It's time," Powell said.

"As planned?"

"As planned."

The taller man pushed to his feet and ran quietly across the last forty yards of open ground. He hunkered down to the left of one of the first floor windows.

Lee followed, kneeling to the right of the same two-foot-wide glass pane. He put his face to the glass, peered inside. There were no draperies to obstruct his view. The canvas blind was halfway raised. Yet the chamber beyond was so intensely dark that it revealed nothing of itself.

"The satchel," Doug said. His voice was not even as loud as the wind.

Opening the bag, Lee set it on the earth between them.

Powell rummaged in it and lifted out a suction cup with a six-inch diameter, a roll of electrician's tape, and a cheap glass cutter approximately twice as large as a church key. He arranged these things before him, in the snow. He looked at his watch. "Ten minutes to eleven," he whispered. "We'll be inside on the hour. With any luck at all, we'll be done and gone by twelve thirty."

Lee nodded and looked around at the campus. He almost expected to see uniformed men moving in on them.

But he saw no one.

There *was* some danger that they would be discovered at this stage, before they got anywhere near the computer terminal. If the motorized university police drove down from the huge men's dormitories on the crest of the hill, they were sure to spot Doug as he cut away the window. The two-lane campus road looped in front of the Institute. The cops could never drive around it and away without spotting them.

Staring at the shadows out there, Lee began to see movement where there was none. (Could that be a man kneeling behind those three, clustered birch trees? And another man lying on the grass on the far side of the road?) He even imagined that he could define the sinister shape of a patrol car which, he further imagined, was descending the hill, its lights switched off and its occupants already alerted to their presence. He squeezed his eyes shut. He had enough to worry about without conjuring up phantoms. Halloween night, indeed. Turning his back on the open grounds, he watched Doug work on the window.

Powell pressed the suction cup firmly to the middle of the lower half of the eight-foot-high window. Next, he used the glass cutter to score the pane all the way across the bottom, a sharp horizontal slice that was close against the metal frame. Moving nimbly despite the cold air, he made a four-foot vertical cut up the left-hand edge of the window, and a matching cut up the right side. Four feet above the first incision he had made, he drew a second horizontal line and joined the two longer cuts.

Where, Lee wondered, had Doug learned this sort of thing? Certainly not in the Army. And not at college. Had he picked it up from Dunio, as he had other things? Was this another skill that was required of a smuggler—and of a smuggler's assistant?

Powell dropped the cutter and reached into the satchel again. He produced a small aluminum bottle equipped with an all-aluminum, manual aerosol device in its screw-on cap. "Acid," he told Lee. "It works on the silicate molecules in the cross-sections of glass I exposed with the cutter. Using this crap, I can be sure the cuts I made are burned all the way through."

Lee was amazed. He could only nod.

Powell made certain that the valve in the miniature metal plunger was turned away from his face, and then he sprayed over every inch of the four lines he had drawn in the window. He put the bottle down in the snow. When a full minute had passed, he gripped the handle on the back of the suction cup, pulled, and snapped loose a three-foot by four-foot section of glass, precisely half of the long window. He slid that across the snow, out of his way.

"Double thickness," he whispered, softly tapping his index finger against a second, inner pane like the one he had just removed.

"You expected that?" Lee asked.

Powell nodded. "Have to be careful here. This one has alarm tape running around the edges. I won't be able to cut right up next to the frame."

"How long?"

"Not long. Don't worry."

Lee broke the promise he had made to himself. He turned and stared again at the night campus behind them.

No one.

He shivered involuntarily.

Powell broke out another section of glass, this one from the inner window, a piece slightly smaller than that which he had carved from the outer pane. He dropped it on the grass, pulled the suction cup from it. Lengths of electrician's tape dangled from one edge, the flexible hinge that had kept the glass from falling into the room beyond.

Time to move.

Lee eased himself through the breached window and into the Recard Institute. It was warmer inside by at least forty degrees. The air smelled of chalk dust and floor wax. He took the satchel when Doug handed it through the window, and he stepped back as the tall man came into the room.

For a long moment, neither of them spoke.

The window blind began to slap in the wind which swept through the holed glass. It sounded as loud as a series of gunshots. Lee grabbed the cord and raised the blind until it was above the inrushing air and would remain still.

Silence returned.

Lee listened to his heart quiet down.

"We better get going," Powell said.

He took a pencil flashlight from his coat pocket. He had taped over three-quarters of the tiny lens. When he switched it on, only the thinnest beam of light shone out into the room. He played it over the walls and furniture.

They were in a large room which contained a dozen draftsmen's tables, an equal number of high padded stools, a wastecan beside each stool, and a dozen wheeled cabinets which were filled and hung with draftsmen's tools. A cone-hooded lamp dangled over each big, slanted drawing table. There was also a teacher's desk, blackboard, and other paraphernalia of a university classroom.

"This is where they teach computer design and electronic draftsmanship," Powell said, quietly. "I remember this. We go through the door and turn left. The night watchman's station should be just this side of the first floor lobby."

"If he's out making his rounds, up on another level—what then?"

"We wait for him to come back."

As Powell switched off the light and started for the classroom door, Lee said, "Wait. The masks."

Powell stopped and fumbled in the inside pocket of his coat.

Lee took out his own mask, a full-face goblin which Carrie had purchased two days ago in a theatrical shop in Manhattan. Since he was wearing tightly fitted pigskin gloves, he found the rubber mask difficult to work with. He put down the satchel, used both hands. After a minute of struggle, he had it in place. Now, every breath smelled of latex.

"I have to switch on the flashlight," Powell said. "I can't tell for sure if I've got the eyeholes where they belong."

When the dim light came on, Lee looked at the other man and saw a grinning, fanged vampire. "It really is Halloween."

"What did you say?" Doug asked.

"Never mind."

He flicked off the flashlight. His rubber fangs glowed green in the dark.

Lee opened the classroom door, and they went out into the corridor, looked left and right. No one was in sight. Only the middle of the three overhead fluorescent strips was turned on, but there was sufficient light for them to see that the long hall was empty.

They went left, walking side by side. Both men held their revolvers out in front of them, as if they were operating one-handed dowsing rods. They were less than fifty feet from the first floor lobby when a door swung open suddenly on their left, and the watchman walked out into the hall.

He was tall, soft-shouldered, big-bellied, a man in his late fifties who had been hard and tough thirty years ago. He was wearing a blue uniform with a matching cap and a holster high on the waist on the left side. He was so surprised to see them that his mouth actually fell open.

"Don't move," Doug Powell said, continuing to come up on him. He centered his gun on the guard's gut.

Tottering backwards, the watchman grabbed for his own revolver. But he quickly thought better of it and reluctantly lifted his hands.

"Very good," Powell said.

"Whatever you jokers have in mind," the watchman said, "you won't get away with it."

Powell burst into laughter. To Lee, he seemed almost hysterical.

10.

Lee realized that the watchman was neither as stupid nor as soft as he had first appeared to be. Beneath his beer belly and sagging jowls, he was grizzled and mean. His eyes were bracketed by leathery folds of flesh, his mouth by grim lines.

Furthermore, he was obviously filled with pride and loath to surrender any of it. He was the type who would have been a football tackle in high school, ass-busting sergeant in the army, and a real bastard in a police uniform. When his pride was threatened, he might do something foolish.

As Doug took the gun out of the guard's holster, Lee said, "What's your name?"

The guard glared at the Colt in Lee's hand. "Rickart."

"First name?" Lee asked.

The guard frowned. "John."

"John, I know you're not a man who can easily accept a thing like this. You aren't used to letting anyone get the jump on you. Right this minute, you're pissed off at us and at yourself. But it's happened, and you've got to make the best of it." Lee saw that his tone and concern were having some effect. "No one's going to think less of you because we got the drop on you. We outnumbered you, that's all. We had more guns."

Gradually, the watchman relaxed. Some of the brittleness went out of him, and his face took on color once more.

"Are we done chatting?" Powell asked sarcastically.

"Take it easy," Lee said.

"Time's running out," Powell said.

"No. We're doing O.K."

They walked Rickart down the corridor to a small, windowless room full of janitorial supplies. There, they made him lie down in the center of the floor, in front of a row of barrels containing cleaning fluids, waxes, and dusting compounds. While Powell stood guard, Lee used the big roll of electrician's tape to bind Rickart's wrists behind his back. Then he took off the watchman's shoes and socks, taped together his bare ankles.

"I can handle him now," Lee said. "You go ahead."

"You know where to find me when you're finished here?" Doug asked. Without waiting for an answer, he said, "Second floor." Then he was gone.

Lying on his well-cushioned stomach as Lee did a better job with a second taping of his hands, Rickart said, "You're both out of your minds."

"Probably," Lee admitted.

"What could you want in this place?"

Lee did not respond.

But Rickart was trying to figure it out to satisfy his own curiosity. "I mean, there's no money, jewels, furs—no *anything.*"

Lee wound a loop of tape around Rickart's calves, to keep him from bowing his legs and breaking the tape at his ankles.

Rickart worried about it. "You sure don't seem like a couple of kids who just broke in to vandalize the place."

"You're right about that, John. That's one thing we aren't," Lee said. "We aren't vandals."

The watchman twisted his head around and rolled his eyes, caught a glimpse of the goblin mask. "Well then, who *are* you? What do you want?"

"Right now," Lee said, "I just want to gag you and then join my friend upstairs. You won't try to bite me, will you?"

Rickart fought it for a moment, then realized that he could only lose no matter how much he prolonged the struggle. He glared at the eyeholes in the goblin mask. Lee used four strips of tape to seal his mouth.

In a seemingly endless monologue, Wilbur Harttle explained that he was a full professor of English literature at Langhorn University, as well as the advisor to the leading fraternity on campus and the consultant to the editorial staff of the school newspaper. He was thirty-nine, married to a frigid bitch named Mary Ellen, had been to Europe four times, owned a Jaguar 2+2 for which he had mortgaged his youth, and was as drunk as a goat. "But I don't think *you're* drunk," he said. "You don't even look like you've had anythin' at all to drink." Her abstinence seemed to strike him as insult.

"I haven't," Carrie said, desperately searching for some way to get rid of him.

"Well, no *wonder* you find the party boring," he said, reaching out to pat her shoulder.

She drew back.

He apparently did not notice her distaste, because he leaned closer. "Why don't you and me go back in there and get a couple of big old vodka martinis?"

"No, thank you."

"Come on," he said, hooking his fingers in her coat sleeve and tugging at her.

"No, really."

He leaned even closer, staring fiercely at her in the weak light. "Grace, you know what?"

"What?"

"I don't think you like me."

She was about to assure him that he was a fine and noble man and that she adored him, when she realized that here might be the way to get him out of the car. "If you want the truth," she said nastily, "I don't think you're at all my type."

"I knew it!" he said. "You're still angry because I made that pass at you." He burped, excused himself. "Although I swear I really wasn't makin' any pass at all."

"It's not that," she said. "I don't much care for drunkards. That's all."

Harttle nodded furiously. "Me either. I—Hey! You think I'm a drunkard?"

"Aren't you?" she asked disdainfully.

"Oh, no!" he said earnestly. "But this is New Year's Eve, for God's sake!" He let go of her sleeve, turned and switched on the radio.

"What are you doing?"

"*Ssshh.*" He tuned in one of the many radio programs designed for the special holiday. "Hear that? Know who that is? Guy Lombardo. When else you ever hear good old Guy Lombardo, except New Year's Eve? Rest of the year, they sew his lips shut and put pennies on his eyes and slip him back into the coffin." He hummed a few bars of the pop waltz which was playing. "New Year's Eve is the wrong time altogether to try to judge if a man's a drunkard. *Everyone's* a drunkard tonight."

She was not going to be able to make him angry. He was one of those on whom booze worked only a benevolent change.

"Want to dance?" he asked.

"Dance?"

"Yeah," he said, sitting up straight and grinning. "We could open the doors, turn the radio up real loud, and dance out on the sidewalk."

"I don't think so," Carrie said. "If you want to dance, you better go back to the party."

"Nah," he said, slumping down again. "I like it better here with you. So we won't dance. We'll just sit here."

"Won't Mary Ellen wonder where you are?" Carrie asked.

"Who?"

"Your wife."

"Oh, her," Harttle said.

"Yes, her."

He laughed. "Hell, let her wonder. I don't care. It'll do her good if she worries about me for a while. Maybe she'll learn not to take me for granted."

Several months after Lee had begun psychotherapy, Dr. Slatvik had suggested that there might be a connection between his impotency and the overwhelming sense of powerlessness which he had developed in Vietnam. He had come to think of himself as a game piece which would be moved around the board according to the whims of a player over whom he had absolutely no control, nor even any meager influence. In joining the Veterans Against the War and participating in the peace demonstrations, he had been attempting to cast off and take command of the forces which he felt had mastered him. However, the VAW and the demonstrations had not changed anything; the war rolled on. His efforts were fruitless, and his feeling of powerlessness only grew. Perhaps, Slatvik had continued, if he could regain confidence in his own ability to shape his fate, he would discover that his impotency was no longer unconquerable.

As Lee closed the door to the storage room where he had bound and gagged the night watchman, self-confidence and *power* began to trickle back into him. For the first time in years, Lee Ackridge felt a measure of personal dignity return to him.

Smiling behind his rubber mask, he went up the main staircase to the second floor.

Across from the head of the stairs, the sign on the half-open door read:

DATA ACQUISITION
DEFENSE DEPARTMENT LINK:
U.S. GOVERNMENT PUBLIC FILES
Trained Operators Only
RICS Projects Only

Lee pushed open the door all the way and stepped into a room which measured forty feet on a side. Somehow, the air itself seemed subterranean here. Although the room was on the second floor, it had no windows. The ceiling was low, squares of white and randomly porous acoustical tile. On every side the walls were lined with filing cabinets full of program cards, storage racks of mag tapes, computer consoles, TV display screens, and the latest model teleprinters. It looked like an underground command center in a movie about nuclear warfare.

"You took care of our dear friend John Rickart?" Doug asked. He was sitting in a spring-backed chair in front of one of the consoles, and he had swiveled around to look at Lee.

"He's not going to be any trouble."

Doug laughed. "He'd like to be. Congratulations on the way you handled him. Very neat. I'd have ruffled his feathers and maybe had to hurt him."

Lee nodded.

"You can take off your mask," Powell said, grinning broadly.

He had pulled down his own vampire face. It hung on an elastic strap from his neck, as if it were sinking fangs into his chest.

Lee pulled off his own mask.

"Come here," Powell said. "I want to show you something."

Lee crossed the room to the primary computer console and stood beside Doug's chair. "Is anything wrong?"

"No, no. Everything is *right. Perfect!*" Powell's brighteyed happiness was disquieting. He was not merely pleased; he was manic.

Keep an eye on him, Carrie had warned. Was she right?

Nonsense. He had spent eleven months in Asia with this man, the closest friend he'd ever known. Doug was just nervous. It was nothing more than that.

"I've opened a line to the Pentagon computer," Powell said.

A warm shiver of excitement passed through Lee.

"I'd like to run a little demonstration for you," Powell said.

"Demonstration?"

Powell pointed to a spiral-bound notebook which lay on the writing surface beside the elaborate console panel. "I've used the Recard Institute's book of data addresses to locate a bit of unclassified material that ought to be fun."

Lee could not understand why they were wasting their time with the unclassified information which was available to any researcher. They had broken into the Institute expressly to steal top secret data. "Fun? What do you mean?"

Clearing his throat on the first word, Doug said, "Naturally, this Defense Department system is capable of running circuitry checks on itself to determine if it's functioning properly. It can ascertain the state of two million of its components in less than three seconds. Nearly any advanced computer can do that." He sat with both hands poised over the dozens of buttons on the console; he looked like a typist ready to begin work. Except that a typist usually did not wear gloves in the office. "But this DD system can also run studies of the theory and practice behind its own design and construction. In other words . . . Well, to popularize it: The DD system can just about psychoanalyze itself as well as give itself a medical examination. Its data banks are full of programs that are concerned with its own analysis of its purpose, functions, accessibility, liability, reliability . . ."

"Okay," Lee said. "I sort of understand. You can ask it questions about itself."

"Precisely," Powell said. "Now . . . I've just tapped the program which deals with the computer's reliability in the handling and dissemination of top secret files. This was an exercise that was conceived by a couple of girls in my class when I was at Recard. It's unclassified stuff; therefore, we can have it all projected on the screens." He indicated a row of three TV displays, each twelve inches square, which were set into the wall above the console. "My questions will appear on the left. The computer's answers will show up on the middle screen."

"And even though it's unclassified," Lee said, "this has a bearing on what we came here to do?"

"Call it an interesting prelude," Powell said.

"Go ahead."

Powell consulted the spiral notebook, studied the program for a moment. He punched buttons.

On the left-hand screen, white letters appeared against a fuzzy green background:

> HALSEY-BRETT EXERCISE
> 33/4/5692/22
> SECURITY DATA REQUESTED
> AT RANDOM

Almost in the same instant that the final word appeared on the left-hand screen, a one-word response rose on the adjoining TV display:

PROCEED

"Now the first question," Powell said. He punched some more buttons, wiping the screen and feeding a data request to the computer. On the left:

WHAT IS THE POSSIBILITY
AND THE PROBABILITY
THAT UNAUTHORIZED PERSONS MIGHT
OBTAIN CLASSIFIED MATERIAL
FROM DD BANKS?

The response was brief but adamant:

POSSIBILITY 00.00001
PROBABILITY ZERO

Powell looked up at Lee and laughed. "Pretty damn sure of itself, isn't it?" He turned to stare at the screen again. "Well, it isn't the poor machine's fault. It's limited by the concepts of the people who program it." He punched more buttons, wiped the screens.

On the left, more letters appeared:

WHAT SECURITY PRECAUTIONS
JUSTIFY THE ASSUMPTION OF
THIS ORDER OF POSSIBILITY
AND PROBABILITY?

Lee had been somewhat disconcerted by the computer's certainty that classified material could not be obtained by someone without security clearance. He watched with interest as the print-out flashed across the middle screen.

LIST OF SECURITY PRECAUTIONS

START LIST:
FIRST TWO ITEMS:
ITEM ONE: SECURITY FILES ARE
MAINTAINED IN SEPARATE BANKS OF
A DIFFERENT MODE FROM UNCLASSIFIED
FILES
ITEM TWO: SECURITY FILES ARE NOT
ACCESSIBLE BY USE OF THE SAME
BINARY LANGUAGE WHICH KEYS
UNCLASSIFIED FILES

"Are you following this?" Powell asked.

"Pretty much," Lee said.

The middle display glowed for a moment, then wiped itself clear. The print-out continued at the top of the cleared screen.

LIST OF SECURITY PRECAUTIONS

CONTINUE LIST:
ITEMS THREE AND FOUR:
ITEM THREE: ADDRESSES TO SECURITY
DATA ARE CODED POSSESSION OF
THE CODES IS LIMITED TO NINE PERSONS
WHO ARE CLEARED FOR TOP SECRET DATA
ITEM FOUR: DD SYSTEM IS EQUIPPED
LOCK-IN ALARM AS AN ALERT THAT
SECURITY DATA HAS BEEN REQUESTED

WITHOUT PRIOR USE OF PROPER
CODE WORDS

After the last line printed, the message held for six seconds, then was automatically wiped. The print-out continued at the top of the screen.

"This could take all night," Powell said. He tapped buttons and erased the screens again, asked the computer another question which it was programmed to answer.

HOW MANY ITEMS ARE IN THE LIST
OF SECURITY PRECAUTIONS?

On the middle screen:

TWENTY–FOUR ITEMS

Powell smiled. Speaking to the TV display rather than to Lee, he said, "But not one of those twenty-four will do you any good tonight." He wiped the screens, punched out another question, the same question he had first asked:

WHAT IS THE POSSIBILITY
AND THE PROBABILITY
THAT UNAUTHORIZED PERSONS MIGHT
OBTAIN CLASSIFIED MATERIAL
FROM DD BANKS?

As expected, the middle screen carried the same answer that it had given the first time:

POSSIBILITY 00.00001
PROBABILITY ZERO

"I feel as if I'm going up against God," Lee said. If the demonstration had been meant to amuse him, it had failed. Instead, he had lost most of the self-confidence which he had only recently begun to enjoy.

Powell blanked the two screens. "Don't let this stuff scare you. Those twenty-four security precautions aren't worth a damn if the wrong person has the code words." He grinned sardonically. "And the wrong person has them."

Lee wiped one hand across his face, recoiled slightly from the feel of the scar tissue on his right cheek. He could still smell the rubber mask as if it were flat against his nostrils. "What was that item about a locked-in alarm?"

"If it's tripped, it goes off in Washington, not here," Doug explained. "But you don't have to worry. We aren't going to trip it. *We have the code words.*"

"O.K.," Lee said. "We've come this far. We have to go ahead with it."

"Of course we do," Powell said. He faced the console again and consulted a folded sheet of paper which he had earlier removed from his shirt pocket; this was the information he had copied from his father's code book. He began to punch buttons. "Watch the tapes," he said.

On Lee's left, four reels of special magnetic tape were fitted onto horizontal spindles in a glass-fronted recording case as large as a refrigerator. All of the reels were motionless.

Powell stopped his manipulation of the console.

Around them, the telecomp center came alive with clickings and clackings, electronic noises.

One of the tapes began to turn.

At the console Powell tapped more buttons.

A second tape began to spin.

A third, too.

Powell got up from the console and stripped off his heavy winter coat.

"It's coming in now?" Lee asked. "The classified files you wanted?"

"You know it."

"It was that easy?"

Powell laughed. "I told you, didn't I? It's coming in on a direct transference line from the Pentagon, off one set of reels onto another."

"And no alarm ringing in Washington?"

"If we'd triggered an alarm, the data wouldn't be feeding onto our tapes. And you can see how beautifully it *is* feeding: thousands and thousands of useful facts every minute."

"I'll be damned."

"No," Powell said. "You'll be *rich.* We're going to pull off the first space-age robbery—using one computer to steal from another—or one *part* of a computer to steal from another part of it. No rough stuff, no violence."

"We still have to collect the ransom," Lee reminded him.

"You know the plan," Powell said. "You know it can be done."

Lee Ackridge nodded and for the second time smiled.

At midnight, the noise from the house on the corner increased at least threefold. Revelers began to blow on party horns. They shouted, shrieked with laughter. The volume climbed on a stereo recording of "Auld Lang Syne."

Wilbur Harttle, who had not said anything for almost five full minutes, roused himself and stared blearily through the windshield. "What's this?" he asked.

"Midnight," Carrie said.

"So what?"

"It's New Year's Eve, remember?" She hoped he would not fall asleep again. When he was unconscious, there was no hope that she could cajole him into leaving the car.

He slapped his own face in pantomimed surprise. "How about that! Happy New Year, Grace Kelly!" He made a clumsy attempt to kiss her, then collapsed against the seat. "Whew!" A moment later he was snoring.

Carrie looked over at the Langhorn campus. She saw nothing of Lee or Doug. The Recard Institute was mostly dark and looked quite peaceful.

Sliding out from under the wheel so that she could turn more directly toward Harttle, she grabbed the lapels of his coat and began to shake him half-heartedly. "Wilbur? Look, you can't sleep here."

Wilbur slept.

Damn!

She supposed that she should have ordered him out of the car the moment he had sat down. She should have threatened to yell rape, anything to get him to leave her alone. But she had been afraid of causing a scene that would attract someone else. Now, she was stuck with him.

"Come on, boy," she said, shaking him more vigorously. "Wake up! I mean it, now."

Harttle muttered but kept his eyes closed. His mouth had sagged open; except for his snoring, he would have made an exceptionally convincing corpse.

Letting go of his lapels, Carrie gently but repeatedly slapped his face. When he did not stir, when he actually began to snore more loudly than ever, she was far less gentle about it. She delivered several good, solid blows that stung her hand despite the glove she wore. "For God's sake, snap out of it!" she hissed in his ear.

Wilbur slid down even farther in his seat.

What now? Leave him there until Lee and Doug returned?

Have them lift him out and dump him? But what if Harttle woke up and saw them? Would he remember their faces and be able to describe them to the police? And if Harttle did get a good look at Doug and Lee, would Powell be willing to take a chance on him, to let that loose end just dangle? Or would he want to kill Harttle and eliminate the threat that he posed?

Powell would kill him, she realized. Unlike her and Lee, Powell was capable of anything. He might even enjoy murder.

"Wilbur," she said, "I don't much like you. But I don't want to have your death on my conscience."

Wilbur smiled in his sleep.

She looked at the house on the corner. Half a dozen people had come out into the yard to set off firecrackers, but none of them was leaving the party.

Over on the campus, all was dark and unmoving.

"O.K." she said.

She knew what she had to do.

Letting the engine run, she got out of the car and quietly closed the door behind her. She hardly noticed the bite of the cold air against her face. She walked hurriedly around the Impala, through the thick plumes of white exhaust that rose from the tail pipe, and opened the door on the passenger's side.

Wilbur Harttle was still snoring.

She leaned in and grasped him by his suit jacket, wrestled with him until she had slid him to the edge of the front seat. Taking a deep breath, she tugged him the rest of the way and stepped back as he spilled out onto the snowy earth.

He swung his arms at some imaginary adversary, muttered incomprehensibly, and collapsed onto his back. Snoring. Loudly.

"Jesus!" she said.

Bending over, she slipped her hands under his armpits, hooked her fingers and tried to drag him backwards.

He giggled, but he did not wake up.

When she put all her strength into it, she found that she could slide him along quite nicely in the snow. She dragged him fifty feet up the street, away from the Impala, then let go of his arms and stood up straight, gasping for breath.

At the corner house, the people on the front lawn were too busy setting off new strings of firecrackers to notice her and what she was doing.

She looked up and down Ox Lane.

Nothing. No one.

She rolled Harttle out of the grass and snow, onto the bare sidewalk where he would surely be discovered before he could die of exposure.

"Sorry Wilbur," she whispered. "That's as much as I can do for you."

Her chest ached. Her heartbeat pounded in her ears. She ran back and climbed into the car.

As Lee packed the six reels of magnetic tape in a cardboard box, which he had gone to the downstairs supply room to retrieve, Doug put the last of their ransom demands on the teleprinter to the Defense Department computer in the Pentagon. Laughing triumphantly, he stood up, pushed the spring-backed chair out of his way, and struggled into his coat. "Are you ready?"

"You're finished?" Lee asked.

"Seems anti-climactic, doesn't it?"

"A bit, yes."

"Remember that right now someone in the receiving room at the Pentagon is reading that ransom demand. Maybe he's not ready to believe it yet. But he'll check it out. In half an hour, this place will be crawling with cops. In an hour, this campus will have more FBI agents than it does trees."

"Actually," Lee said, "it's all just beginning."

They left the lights on, went down the main stairs and back the first floor corridor to the classroom where they had broken into the Recard Institute. They went out through the window which Doug had earlier cut away.

The night was just as cold and black as it had been an hour and a half ago.

Halloween. Definitely Halloween, Lee thought as they made their way toward Ox Lane.

Yet Doug had shown no fear through any of it. He had never once turned to stare over his shoulder. He had not paused, as Lee had, to listen for pursuit. He was too sure of himself.

At the edge of the campus, they waited for a lone car to pass along Ox Lane, then they crossed over to the Impala.

Carrie was waiting for them. She kissed Lee on his unscarred left cheek and looked at the reels in the box which he held on his lap. "You did it!" she said.

"We did it," Lee agreed, with mixed emotions.

"Oh, sister, did we *ever* do it!" Doug Powell said.

"Are you O.K.?" Lee asked. "Any trouble?"

Carrie smiled. "Me? All I had to do was sit and wait."

11.

In the bedroom of his town house on G Street in Washington, Roy Genelli was having a most pleasant dream. It was all about a family reunion. Apparently, it was *his* family's reunion, although it was peopled by relatives whom he had never known. The gathering was out in the country somewhere, on the edge of a very Frostian New England wood. Long picnic tables were set under the trees and covered with white cloths, laden with food. Beer was on tap, and cases of Coke rested on tubs full of ice. There were many people of all ages . . . He wandered among them, talking baseball and politics, discussing other relatives, jobs, movies they had seen, television shows . . . Everybody was happy and close and loving, and they all stopped talking when the telephone rang inside one of the picnic hampers.

The telephone rang a second time, destroying the dream altogether. There was no way he could rationalize the presence of a telephone in a picnic hamper.

He sat up in bed and lifted the receiver. "Hello."

"Roy?"

"Speaking."

"This is Peterson." Gardner Peterson, of course. He was the only man Roy knew who could comfortably refer to himself by his last name.

"Mr. Peterson?" He kept his eyes closed, hoping against hope that he would not wake up all the way.

"Did I wake you?"

As special assistant to the supervisor of the Middle-Eastern District of the Federal Bureau of Investigation, Genelli answered to the district supervisor himself, Gardner Peterson. Although he and Peterson had worked together almost daily for fifteen years, they shared absolutely no social relationship or off-duty friendship. In all those years, Peterson had never telephoned Roy Genelli at his home. Now, in the middle of the night, in the middle of one of the nicest dreams imaginable, the bastard had to . . .

"Roy? Are you there?"

"Yes, sir," Genelli said. He opened his eyes and leaned over in bed to stare closely at the clock on the nightstand.

The irradiated dial read 1:10. In the morning? Had to be in the morning.

"Roy—"

"I've been asleep for a couple of hours. I'm not tracking too well right now. Forgive me if I—"

"That's okay," Peterson assured him. "Take your time. I'm just glad I got hold of you. I was afraid you'd be out celebrating." The relief in his voice was evident even across the hollow telephone line.

"No celebrations, sir. I work tomorrow."

"New Year's Day?"

Peterson had been drinking heavily, or he would have remembered that detail.

"I nearly always work on holidays," Genelli said. He put a hand to his mouth and stifled a yawn.

"That's right, of course," Peterson said. He paused, took a deep breath in the fashion of a man about to leap into the deep end of a swimming pool. "Look, you'd better get dressed. I've sent a car around for you. It'll be there in five or ten minutes."

The clinging remnants of the dream whirled away like the last shreds of fog lashed by a morning wind.

Genelli was all at once wide-eyed and alert. He knew that something was terribly wrong. Not only had Peterson broken personal tradition by calling him at home; but this was the first time that Genelli had ever rated a chauffeured car. "What's the situation, sir?"

"Desperate," Peterson said without a hint of humor. "I want you to work as my deputy on a case that's just broken here."

"I went off duty at six o'clock," Genelli said. "There was nothing happening then that would—"

"I know," Peterson said impatiently. "It broke only forty minutes ago."

Forty minutes?

In his twenty years with the Bureau, Genelli had never seen an all-out investigation launched within forty minutes of the first case report. Except, of course, for the assassination of John Kennedy. That day, the red tape had been quickly snipped, and men were in the field within twenty minutes of the news break from Dallas. Was that what this was all about? Had someone gotten to another president?

"I'm not fully informed yet myself," Peterson was saying. "I was at a party when the Director called me about twenty or twenty-five minutes ago. Besides, it's most certainly something I can't go into on the telephone, not even for the bare essentials." He sounded more harried than Genelli had ever heard him. "Look, the driver will pick you up and deliver you to a Mr. Ives who'll brief you in detail."

"Where's this?" Genelli asked. "At the Bureau?"

"No," Peterson said. "And I'd prefer not to say where, not on the telephone."

What the hell *was* this? "You can't even tell me where I'm going?" Genelli asked.

"It's like that, yes. And, by the way, the driver's yours until you don't need him anymore."

Genelli frowned. "Thanks."

"I'll see you later."

The line went dead.

Genelli hung up, kicked the covers back, and scrambled out of bed. He stripped off his pajamas, wondering as he fumbled with the drawstring if this were, at last, another Zilinski-Ross case.

He shaved quickly, splashed water in his face, and dressed in under five minutes.

In the walk-in closet, he took his revolver from the shelf. It was not loaded, but he could take care of that in the car. He strapped on the shoulder holster and tucked the .38 into the leather. Pulling on his suit jacket, he dropped a small box of ammunition into his pocket.

When he got downstairs, the government car was waiting for him at the curb. He slid into the back seat and slammed the door.

"Mr. Genelli?" the driver asked. He was young, blond, the kind of FBI man you saw in the movies but seldom encountered in reality.

"Yes, I'm Genelli."

"My name's Plover," the driver said.

"Glad to meet you."

Plover nodded, smiled, and faced front again. He threw the car into gear and left rubber behind them on the pavement.

Genelli regained his balance as the car rocketed down G Street. Leaning forward, he said, "Where are we going?"

"Pentagon," Plover said. "That's all I know, sir."

"Me too," Genelli said.

JANUARY 1, 2:00 A.M.
JANUARY 2, 4:00 P.M.

The Emergency

12.

At the mall entrance to the Pentagon, the taller of the two armed marine guards who met Genelli said, "We're to take you down to Colonel Theodore Ives, on the computer level."

"Fine," Genelli said.

Their hard-heeled boots clicked smartly on the polished floors. They walked so fast that Genelli, who was considerably shorter than either of them, could barely keep up.

They stopped at two checkpoints where Genelli was required to present his Bureau ID. At the first station he surrendered his revolver. At the second station he was issued a set of security tags which he hung around his neck on a fine ball chain.

Before he could board the elevator that would take him to the Pentagon subbasements, Genelli had to stop and sign his name yet again, show his identification one more time, and have his picture taken with a Polaroid camera. He did not smile. Neither did the two uniformed guards who were on duty at the elevator post.

His own marines accompanied him into the elevator. They rode down in silence.

After another walk down another series of immaculate corridors, Genelli was delivered to Colonel Theodore Ives and to a room like no other he had ever seen.

Ives was six-one, thin, with short-cropped hair the color of sand and eyes as gray as pencil smears. He wore a simple khaki army uniform, which was devoid of all decoration except the insignia of his rank. He was cool and brisk, even though he was quite obviously under pressure. But for the slight tic at the right corner of his mouth, he might have been a robot rather than a man.

The room in which Ives worked was considerably more interesting than the man who reigned supreme there. It was full of enormous computer housings, walls of controls, and monitor lights. Lighted scopes pulsed, and there were TV displays in the form of block print, graph, and hologram informational presentations. Teletype machines clattered in one corner. Computer consoles blinked, purred, chattered incessantly. Functional four-way command chairs stood before the equipment, enough of them to accommodate more than forty data technicians. At the moment, due to the extremely sensitive nature of the crisis, most of the technicians had been dismissed. Ives was operating the room with the aid of only two security-cleared subordinates.

"How much do you know about it?" Ives asked, straight off.

"Nothing," Genelli said.

That did not faze the colonel. He led Genelli across the room to an alcove where there was a couch, several chairs, a card table, and a coffee machine. "I'll try to boil it down to something a layman can understand." Without asking if Genelli wanted coffee, Ives dropped dimes into the machine, produced two cupfuls. "Well, in essence, what we have here is the greatest breach of security in the history of the United States. No. Make that read 'in the history of the world.' "

Genelli blew on his coffee. Steam rose up his nose.

"It's the cleverest and most damaging bit of espionage ever directed against this country." Ives was not trying to be melodramatic. He was incapable of exaggeration; he was merely telling the truth as he saw it.

"Domestically initiated espionage," Genelli said. "Otherwise, it would be in the hands of the CIA and the CID."

"Oh, they're being brought into it," Ives said. "The CID is moving agents into this building right now. Every last employee on this floor and on any other level of the Pentagon will be investigated, quietly but thoroughly. And the CIA's burning lights too. A great deal of information was stolen. The CIA is trying to find who in the hell is out there, somewhere in the world, waiting to take it off the hands of the thieves."

"And I'm to find these thieves?"

"You'd damn well better, Mr. Genelli," Ives said. "or else we've all had it."

Genelli put down his unfinished coffee. "Tell me the whole story."

As succinctly as he could, the colonel told Genelli about the DD system, the trunk line terminals which fed into it from all over the country, and the way one of those terminals had been misused. During the half hour required for the explanation, the two aides kept stepping into the alcove to request orders and to report to Ives all urgent developments. After each of these interruptions, the colonel picked up his story precisely where he had stopped. He was an efficient man. Genelli admired him for that.

When he was finished, the colonel said, "Now, you must have some questions."

Genelli had thousands, but he realized that most of them were the same ones to which Ives and his men were seeking answers.

He thought about it for a moment, then said, "Why do you think it was espionage?"

Ives stared at him as if he had opened his mouth and coughed out a bluebird. "For Christ's sake, what else would you call it?"

Genelli shrugged but watched Ives closely as he said, "Maybe it's just what the thieves called it in that note you say they sent on the teleprinter."

"Robbery?"

"That's what they told us," Genelli said. "And they're in a position to know best." He closed his eyes and tried to frame words to fit the situation. "They kidnapped information, and they're holding it for ransom. It's a hijacking of vital data, if you will. Something altogether new."

Ives shook his head. "No. The ransom demand is a cover. It's only meant to get us running off on the wrong trail."

"A red herring works best when you've got only one detective after you," Genelli said. "When every law officer in the country is on your trail, a red herring is useless."

Ives crumpled up the coffee cup that he still held in one hand. "Try to understand. These people, whoever they are, evidently used an electronic device to circumvent, negate, and confuse every one of the two dozen safeguards we have built into the DD system. I can't begin to tell you what that device was or how they used it. Two hours ago, I didn't even believe that anyone without top security clearance could employ the computer like this. But we *will* eventually learn what they did." With a quick snap of his wrist, he threw the ruined paper cup into the wastebasket on the other side of the alcove. "And already it's clear they can't be conventional crooks. The brain power and the resources would be out of the reach of any single man or group of ordinary citizens. Even a bunch of multi-millionaires couldn't reasonably finance it! It would require the concerted efforts of an entire governmental research arm. *That's* why I'm certain it's espionage." The tic at the corner of his mouth was jumping rapidly.

For a long moment Genelli stared into the main room at the busy machines. The colonel's frustration and fear seemed genuine; yet Genelli could not strike the man from any list of suspects. He wanted to give serious thought to the colonel's arguments. However, there was one gaping hole . . . "They didn't need any fancy electronic gadgets," he said, at last. "They needed those code words. That's all."

"I knew you'd come back to that," Ives said.

"It seems logical."

Ives frowned. He plainly disapproved of that theory. "I've told you that only nine people have those code words. And they're fairly respectable people, you must admit. No matter what you think of the people in the White House right now, it's difficult to picture a President or Vice-President embarking on *this* sort of crime."

"There's the Secretary of Defense, Chairman of the Joint Chiefs, and the other service chiefs," Genelli said. "And there's this Dennis Atwell, the Pentagon's liaison with Congress."

"No," Ives said. "It's espionage, pure and simple. We're up against the agents of a foreign government, men who had the use of some advanced electronic tapping device."

"There's you," Genelli said.

"Of course," Ives said sarcastically.

"I'm serious."

"Why in the hell would I—"

"For the money," Genelli said.

Ives glared at him.

"I'll have to put you under surveillance," Genelli said. "And we'll run a full investigation on your background." He looked away from Ives, out at the main room again. "I'd like to see that ransom demand that came in on the teletype."

At the semi-circular command desk in the middle of the large room, Colonel Ives picked up three sheets of paper and gave them to Genelli. "This is only a copy. The original's already in the hands of your Director. But it's sheer nonsense, just something to mislead us."

Genelli read it closely.

MESSAGE XXXXXXXXXX
TIME: 0020 EST
ORIGIN: LANGHORN/RECARD
FROM: ROBIN HOOD
TO: PRESIDENT OF THE UNITED STATES
FOR: YI
SUBJECT: RANSOM DEMAND
EIGHT PART MESSAGE FOLLOWS

MESSAGE BEGINS:
PART ONE: WE ARE HOLDING SIX MAGNETIC TAPES OF HIGHLY CLASSIFIED DATA FOR RANSOM BEFORE YOU DISMISS THIS MESSAGE AS AN ELABORATE HOAX, WE SUGGEST THAT YOU RUN REVELATORY PROGRAM ON THE DD SYSTEM AND DETERMINE WHAT INFORMATION IT PROVIDED TO THE LANGHORN/RECARD TERMINAL WITHIN THE PAST TWO HOURS

PART TWO: WE ARE NOT AGENTS OF A FOREIGN POWER AND ARE IN NO WAY CONNECTED TO THE INTELLIGENCE GATHERING APPARATUS OF ANY OTHER NATION

WE ARE AMERICAN CITIZENS WITH AN ENTREPRENEURIAL SPIRIT OUR PRIMARY MOTIVATION IS MONEY HOWEVER, IN THE EVENT THAT YOU DO NOT MEET OUR DEMANDS OR DO NOT OBSERVE THE CAREFULLY DETAILED ARRANGEMENTS FOR THE PAYMENT OF THE RANSOM, WE WILL DELIVER THESE TAPES TO AN INTERESTED FOREIGN GOVERNMENT THIS IS NO BLUFF OUR SECONDARY MOTIVATION IS TO

PROVE TO THE ARROGANT MILITARY ESTABLISHMENT THAT EVEN THE GREATEST WORLD POWER IS VULNERABLE IN THIS MECHANIZED AGE

PART THREE: ANY ATTEMPT ON YOUR PART TO DELAY THE PAYMENT OF THE RANSOM, OR TO SUBSTITUTE OTHER VALUABLES FOR THOSE WHICH WE DEMAND, WILL BE VIEWED BY US AS A REFUSAL OF COOPERATION ON YOUR PART WE WILL THEN PASS THE TAPES TO A FOREIGN AGENCY THE MESSAGE YOU ARE READING IS THE LAST YOU WILL RECEIVE YOU WILL HAVE NO OPPORTUNITY TO CONVERSE WITH US OR TO BARGAIN FOR OTHER TERMS WITHOUT DELAY, YOU SHOULD BEGIN TO MAKE ARRANGEMENTS TO DELIVER THE RANSOM AS WE HAVE SPECIFIED BELOW NO SECOND CHANCES

Ives interrupted. "It's the most ridiculous thing I've ever read. It's just a pathetic attempt—"

"I'd like to finish it before I comment," Genelli said. He read slowly through the next two pages, perplexed but intrigued by the ransom they wanted and by the plan which they had devised for its payment. When he was finished, he said, "Very neat."

"Still believe they're just crooks?" Ives asked.

"Yes. And I'm wondering why you adamantly refuse to believe it. Is it just military paranoia—or are you trying to confuse the issue?"

Ives blushed.

"Do you know just what data they took?" Genelli asked, before the colonel could continue the argument.

Ives ran one hand through his bristled hair and, for the first time, looked decidedly harried. "We've been working on that. Let's go see what we've learned."

Genelli followed him across the long room to a dial-bedecked, button-studded console that was situated below half a dozen twelve-inch TV displays.

Ives sat in the operator's chair, studied the board, punched buttons, and looked up at the screen.

Immediately in front of them, the print-out flashed in white letters against a green background:

LANGHORN/RECARD
MOST RECENT DATA REQUESTS
LISTED BY GENERAL SUBJECT AREA;
SPECIFIC DATA AVAILABLE
GENERAL SUBJECTS ONLY:

ONE: CURRENT WEAPONS RESEARCH
AND DEVELOPMENT/ UNITED STATES/
ALL PROGRAMS/ ALL DETAILS

TWO: CIA OPERATIVES/ ALL NATIONS/
ALL DETAILS

THREE: BATTLEFIELD STRATEGIES/
ALL POTENTIAL CONFLICTS/ ALL
DETAILS

"It's going to be as bad as possible," Colonel Ives said. "It's going to be disastrous." He was speaking more to himself than to Genelli.

The computer continued.

FOUR: CURRENT WEAPONS RESEARCH
AND DEVELOPMENT/ SOVIET UNION/
ALL KNOWN DETAILS/ ALL SOURCES

FIVE: MERCENARIES EMPLOYED BY
UNITED STATES/ WORLDWIDE/ ALL
NAMES/ ALL PAST AND CURRENT
OPERATIONS/ ALL DETAILS

SIX: TRANSLATION OF DD SYSTEMS
PROGRAM/ DECODED/ FULL

SPECIFIC DATA AVAILABLE
CALL FOR ADDITIONAL DISPLAY

They stared at the screen as the last two lines of the print-out blinked on and off, on and off, like a string of Christmas tree bulbs.

"Do you want a more specific breakdown of what was stolen?" Ives asked. His voice had risen a few tones, and he had aged considerably in the last five minutes. If his patriotic concern was an act, it was a good one.

"Yes," Genelli said. "But not now. I don't have time now. I'll send someone around for that data later."

"They didn't steal just random data," Ives said, incredulous. "They knew exactly what they were after."

Genelli's voice was lower and harder than it had been. "You say there are only nine code books?"

"Yes," the colonel said. "But—"

"Do they all contain the same thing?"

"Excuse me?"

"The same thing," Genelli snapped. "Do they all contain the same codes?"

"There's never more than one operative code word for each of the classified data categories," Ives said.

"That's not quite what I asked," Genelli said. "What I meant was . . . You said there are fifty data categories?"

Ives nodded.

"Does every one of those nine books contain all fifty code words —as well as the hundreds of data addresses which you described to me?"

"No," Ives said.

"Explain."

"Not every man who receives the bi-weekly code changes has a legitimate reason for tapping all of the fifty subject banks. For instance, none of the heads of the three services would have occasion to call for data on the CIA. Neither would the Secretary of Defense. Some of these books contain as few as fifteen code words, cover only fifteen categories. We operate on a need-to-know basis."

Genelli smiled. He had suspected as much. "In other words, those books could not be used to obtain data from the CIA file that was stolen tonight?"

"That's correct," Ives said. He did not see what Genelli was getting at, and he was growing impatient.

"Are any of the code books complete?"

"With all fifty words and a full list of salient data addresses?" Ives asked. "Yes. Three of them have the whole thing."

"Which three?"

"President, Chairman of the Joint Chiefs—and me."

Genelli was surprised. "The Chairman of the Joint Chiefs has the full deal, but the Vice-President does not?"

"In the past," Ives said, "only the President and I had all of it. But when he appointed General Powell to be the new Chairman of the Joint Chiefs two years ago, the President asked me to prepare a third, full code book."

"Why?"

"Well . . . The President uses Powell as a close, probably his closest, advisor as well as his direct link to the military."

Clearly, the colonel questioned the wisdom of preparing a complete, all-categories code book for General Powell.

"Do you think Powell is unreliable?" Genelli asked.

Ives hesitated.

"Well?"

"Not necessarily," the colonel said. "It's just that the more copies of the full code that are floating around, the greater the chance that something can go wrong."

"And has. But you have no reason to suspect Powell?"

"Of course not."

"Naturally," Genelli said, "you're the most likely suspect."

Ives bristled. "Look—"

"*Are* you behind this?" Genelli asked.

Ives's face grew red. "In all my years—"

"No speeches, please," Genelli said. "I gave you a chance. If you *are* involved, you'll wish you'd taken it. In any event, I'll be getting back to you in twelve hours to see if you've come up with anything more." He smiled coldly and turned away from Ives. He walked briskly across the room to the door before the colonel could respond.

The two armed marine guards were waiting for him in the brightly lighted corridor.

The taller of them said, "Mr. Gardner Peterson and two other gentlemen are waiting for you upstairs, sir. Corridor Six, E Ring." By the way he said it, Corridor Six of E Ring was VIP territory.

"Let's go, then," Genelli said.

He wanted to talk to Peterson anyway. He wanted to ask for certain men, equipment, authorizations . . . They had no time to waste. If they were going to meet the ransom demand, they did not even have two days to solve this thing.

Genelli did not mind the time limitations that the thieves' ransom conditions imposed upon him. In fact, he thrived on that sort of crisis situation.

Fourteen years ago, when they had been trying to nail Zilinski and Ross before those two maniacs murdered someone else, hadn't he been involved in a race against time? Yes. And he had won it, too.

On the way up in the elevator, Roy Genelli began to whistle.

The smaller marine turned to stare at him.

The tall one looked straight ahead, as if he were deaf.

13.

The office in E Ring was large, richly carpeted, and expensively furnished straight from an Ethan Allen catalogue. It must have belonged, Genelli thought, to at least an under-secretary of one of the services, and probably to a secretary himself. The heavy blue drapes were drawn shut at both windows. The only light came from a lamp on the over-sized desk. The corners of the room were in darkness, while shadows trembled on the edges of everything else.

Gardner Peterson was sitting behind the desk. He was a tall, broad-shouldered man who had begun his last decade of FBI work; when he was sixty-two, he would retire with a forty-year pension. Unless, of course, the present Director died or resigned and Peterson was asked to replace him. He was not handsome, but certainly distinguished. His gray hair was more stylishly cut than was usual for an FBI man, and he dressed well. He did not stand up when Genelli entered the room, but motioned to a vacant chair which faced the desk.

The other two chairs were already occupied.

As he sat down, Genelli recognized one of the other men. He smiled and nodded at David Meyrowitz. Meyrowitz was his first choice for an assistant. In the course of previous cases, he had proved to be an invaluable, imaginative aide. Genelli had been prepared to make that clear to Peterson; as usual, the supervisor was one step ahead of him.

On second glance, Genelli found that the man in the third easy chair was not the complete stranger he had at first seemed to be. They had never met before, but Genelli recognized the CIA Director even before Peterson had the opportunity to make the introductions.

They reached out from their chairs, stretching across Meyrowitz's lap, and shook hands.

"I'm not horning in on the FBI's turf," the Director said, with a smile that was not at all convincing. "But my people are limited to out-of-country work. And this thing is unfolding right here at home. I want to know what's happening on your front, so I can better coordinate my own agents overseas. They might have to move fast when you discover where those tapes are going to be delivered. I suppose the FBI's stake in this is no larger than ours."

"No, sir," Genelli said. "I'm afraid the CIA has a great deal *more* at stake than we do. Colonel Ives just located the specific data that was stolen. One of the tapes is a full file on the CIA operative staff."

The color drained from the Director's face.

"You might as well tell us the rest of it," Peterson said.

Genelli went through it quickly, giving them a rough summary of what Ives had told him.

The CIA man had time to regain his composure. When Genelli was done, the Director said, "You've read that teletype message they put through from Langhorn?" He pointed to a copy of the three-page ransom demand which lay on the desk.

"Yes," Genelli said.

Leaning forward, his elbows on the arms of his chair and his thick-fingered hands gripping his knees, the Director said, "What do you think? Is it an attempt to cover their tracks? Or is it the genuine article?"

Genelli settled back in his chair and tried to relax. He knew he might have to sell them on his intended approach to the case, and he wanted to appear completely sure of himself. "I think they are what they say they are."

"Just thieves," Peterson said.

"Yes."

Peterson picked a pencil from the holder that stood on the corner of the blotter, unconsciously began to play with it, rolling it between his hands. "Why do you think they *aren't* enemy agents, Roy?"

Genelli was ready for that one. "For one thing, if enemy agents had broken into Langhorn and pulled this off, they wouldn't have bothered to toss out a red herring. Especially not one as fantastic as this. At most, they'd try to direct our attention away from their own people and toward another nation that wasn't involved. But I just can't see them concocting this ransom story."

"But we must cover other possibilities too," Peterson said.

"Of course," Genelli agreed. "You'll put men on all the foreign diplomats and embassy workers in the country. We already have routine twenty-four hour tails on the most dangerous ones . . . All I'm saying is that I'd like to step out of the role of your chief coordinator on this. I want out of the office and in the field. I'm the best man you've got for shaping and directing the major facet of this investigation. I want to handle the ransom demand as if it were serious, look for domestic sources and not spies. From the tone of that teletype message—the romantic use of a code name like Robin Hood; the anti-military talk—I'd say we might be dealing with domestic left-wingers. But at this point, that's just speculation."

"We have half a dozen men from the Philadelphia field office over in Langhorn. You'll want to start there?" Peterson asked.

"Yes," Genelli said. "Then I'll want eighty or a hundred men standing by in New York City. The ransom exchange is set there, so these people are probably based in New York. I'll also want twenty men to check out a few special people."

"Who?" the CIA Director asked.

"Colonel Theodore Ives and General Norman Powell, to start."

"Ives is an obvious choice," Peterson said, playing with the pencil. "But the Chairman of the Joint Chiefs?"

"He's the only man besides Ives and the President who has a full code book, the only other man who could have gotten the CIA file."

"Very well," Peterson said. "Anything else?"

"Yes," Genelli said, in full control. "Make arrangements to pay the ransom. If we don't get anywhere by five o'clock tomorrow—and that's just thirty-eight hours from now—we'll try to nail them during the ransom delivery."

"I don't need to make arrangements," Peterson said. "We'll just fill that box with cardboard instead of what they asked for."

Genelli frowned. "If they get away with the box and find they've been tricked, they'll turn those tapes over to the Chinese. Or whoever."

Peterson screwed up his face as if he had just tasted something bitter. "You think if they get what they want, they'll return those tapes like good little boys?"

"There's a good chance of it," Genelli said.

"I agree," Meyrowitz said, speaking for the first time since

Genelli had come into the room. "They know what would happen to the world balance of power if they passed this information to an enemy. Once they've got their money, what does it benefit them to destroy us? They'll want to preserve the system once they're a monied part of it. They'll send the tapes back."

Peterson looked at the CIA man, then at Genelli. "I'll make the preparations."

"Is this stuff they want really worth all that much?" the CIA Director asked.

"I've already looked into that," Peterson said, getting to his feet. "It's worth millions." He turned to Genelli. "I'll be going to New York tonight. You'll have your men when *you* get there from Langhorn. There's a jet waiting at National to take you to Philly, and there's a second plane waiting there. Anything else?"

"Not at the moment," Genelli said, eager to be moving.

The time was 3:26 in the morning, New Year's Day.

Plover was waiting in the government Ford when they came out of the Mall Exit. He accelerated out of the Pentagon drive and headed toward the nearby National Airport.

Genelli began to whistle again.

"No reason to be so happy," Meyrowitz said. "Don't you see the ax?" He pointed over Genelli's head as if the instrument hung there by a slender thread. There was a rare note of concern under his characteristic flippancy. "If we blow this, they'll need scapegoats. That's you and me."

Genelli stared at him. Meyrowitz was twenty-eight, Genelli's height but hard and wiry as an acrobat. He had the air of a man who could handle anyone and anything. It was not like him to nurture pessimism.

"Neither one of us is in the old WASP tradition of the Bureau. Look at us: a wop and a Jew. Peterson would sacrifice us without a second thought. We aren't two of the boys."

Plover cornered to the right at better than ninety miles an hour. Tires screamed.

When Genelli was upright again, he said, "I don't really care if they bounce me out of the Bureau."

"Oh, I could live without the Bureau," Meyrowitz said. "But there will be Congressional investigations. We'll be on the hot seat, our faces in all the papers. There'll be charges of dereliction of duty . . . You think they railroaded the Rosenbergs? Wait until you see the job they do on us."

"Now, David—"

"This country is going to be crazy-angry if we blow this," Meyrowitz insisted. "And scared shitless. They'll strike out blindly, just to relieve the tension." He stared at Genelli who stared back with the stirrings of doubt in his eyes. "Do you see the ax now?" Meyrowitz asked.

14.

"It's not the end of the world," Carrie said gently.

With all the lights out, they were lying on the bed in the hotel room. The reddish glow of the city's neon seeped through the drapes and softly fired the darkness. They were nude. She was lying with her face pressed against his neck, her lithe body tight against his. He had his arms around her.

He said, "I thought for sure tonight . . ."

"I told you it was too soon," she said tenderly. "You've got too much on your mind. So do I."

For several minutes, neither of them spoke.

A siren wailed in the street below, rose, faded, was gone.

Lee sighed. "You know what I was thinking tonight when I was inside the Recard building? About Slatvik. About what he once said—that my impotency is probably connected to my feeling of powerlessness."

"I remember that."

"Well, I'm no longer powerless. I feel in charge now. So why can't I make it with you?"

"It's too soon," she said. "Be patient."

"That's fine for me. I can try to wait it out, because at this point I don't have anything to lose." He hesitated, then went on with it: "But it's not fair to ask you for more patience, not after all these months."

"Oh, shut up," she said, in the way of good-humored chastisement. "You still think I'm the type who picks up injured baby birds and nurses them back to health. Well, maybe there's a little bit of that instinct in me. And maybe that *is* part of the reason I moved in with you in the first place. But that isn't why I stayed. Dammit, I love you."

He was as moved by the fierceness of her short speech as by what she had said. Yet he continued to feel guilty and ineffectual, because he had not been a man to her. And the guilt spread to other things, pulsed in him larger and larger, like a tumor. "I shouldn't have gotten you into this."

"You didn't. I *wanted* to get into it. I'm responsible for myself. So let's just not talk about that, huh?"

But he could not drop it altogether. "I'm afraid you're right about Doug. He's not himself. I don't know what it is."

"We'll both watch him," she said. She hugged Lee tighter. "If we both watch him, nothing bad can happen. It's two against one. We'll come through this. We'll get the money and never have to worry again. Then, if you need Slatvik, you can pay for his treatment yourself." The way she spoke, it sounded as if she were chanting a litany.

"We're going to make it," he said.

"I know we are."

After several minutes of silence, as if they had never stopped talking about Doug Powell, she said, "We'll both watch him.

Nothing bad can happen if we both watch him every step of the way."

In his own room, Doug Powell paced back and forth beside the bed, waiting for the telephone to ring. He had been waiting ever since four o'clock, when the call had been scheduled to come through.

At 4:18, the phone rang.

He grabbed it. "Hello?"

The hotel operator said, "Mr. Powell?"

"Yes."

"I have a collect call for you from a Mr. Hyde in New York City."

Powell wiped one sweaty palm down his shirt. "Go ahead."

"Will you accept the charges?" the operator asked.

"Put it on my room bill," he said.

A moment later, Ilya Zaitsev said, "Mr. Powell?"

"Hello, Mr. Hyde."

"I'm sorry to inconvenience you, but the most convenient phone was a public booth."

"Of course," Powell said.

Zaitsev spoke perfect English. Since Powell had met him two and a half years ago at a Washington party, the Russian had worked hard to eradicate his accent. "I'm terribly sorry to disturb you at this hour," he said. "But that call came in from Zurich. Your lawyers have arranged everything. Do you wish to consummate the deal as we discussed it some days ago?"

"I certainly do!" Powell said, grinning at the wall in front of him.

Zaitsev was silent a moment. Finally: "Then shall we continue as planned?"

"Just as we talked about it, yes."

"I'll see you tomorrow evening," Zaitsev said.

"Until then."

Both men hung up.

Powell sat down on the edge of the bed. He held his arms straight out and looked at his hands. They were shaking. But it was not fear which caused those tremors. It was excitement. He had already telephoned Dunio. Everything was moving along smoothly; Dunio would have the money ready in time. All that remained to be done before he passed the tapes to Zaitsev was to collect the ransom. The beautiful ransom. That was a final, exquisite slap in the face for the government—the payment of the ransom. It was actually a double slap, because they would choke it up and lose it as well as the tapes. He could barely sit still, thinking about it.

"General Norman Powell," he said aloud. He held up his hands to frame an imaginary headline. "Powell Relieved of Command. Denies Prior Knowledge of Son's Perfidy."

Perfidy? Ah, that was perfect.

He rolled over on the bed, buried his face in the pillows, and giggled.

Sitting in their car on the east side of Central Park West, Agents Ashe and Packer, who constituted the routine midnight-to-eight tail on Ilya Zaitsev, watched the Russian emerge from a sidewalk telephone booth.

"He's going straight back to his apartment," Ashe said.

Lights out, hugging the parked cars, Packer drifted the Bureau car along in Zaitsev's wake.

In three blocks the Russian entered his apartment building.

"Good," Ashe said. "We don't have to chase his ass all over the city."

Packer pulled the unmarked patrol car into a parking slot and switched off the lights. He had been assigned to this duty only last night, and he was still fascinated by it. "What do you think that call was about?"

"Nothing," Ashe said. "He's dull. He came from Russia three years ago, had the manners of a potato farmer. He spent a year building his UN cover. The last two years he's cultivated intelligence sources. Since then, the CIA's been feeding him a lot of phony information which he's passed on to Moscow. He probably knows it's phony. But he's got to keep trying. And the Bureau's got to keep a tail on him in case he gets lucky and hooks up with an informer who *isn't* a CIA ringer."

"Maybe this time, he's got a live wire," Packer insisted.

"We'll put a tap on the phone if he uses it again," Ashe said. "But I can guarantee it's nothing important."

15.

New Year's Day—5:00 P.M.

Roy Genelli's temporary office in the FBI headquarters on East Sixty-ninth Street in Manhattan was not as comfortable as the room where he had met Gardner Peterson in Corridor Six, E Ring of the Pentagon. In fact, it was half the size, with drab institutional green walls, a gray tile floor ungraced by carpeting, and the standard government issue metal office furniture.

The atmosphere did not depress Genelli, for he was hardly aware of any of it. He was too busy working on what had come to be coded as the Robin Hood Case to pay much attention to office decor. He had slept for half an hour on the Air Force jet from Philadelphia to Floyd Bennett Field, and had caught another two hours between twelve and two o'clock this afternoon. Otherwise, he had been going steadily since Peterson's telephone call at 1:10 this morning. The only detail he noticed about the office assigned to him in New York was that it contained a thirty-cup electric percolator and fresh-ground coffee.

He was drinking coffee as if addicted to it.

He was pouring his third cup of the hour when David Meyrowitz walked into the room with a handful of pages from the teleprinter. "What now?"

"More nothing," Meyrowitz said, throwing the papers on the cluttered desk.

"Explain, please."

The younger man came over to the corner table to pour his own coffee. "The field office in Philly just sent through reports on ten more of the guests at that Ox Lane New Year's Eve party." Everyone at the party had been questioned by now. However, not everyone had been given a full-depth background study; but that was steadily proceeding through the efforts of forty agents from the Philadelphia and Baltimore areas. "They're all nice people. The worst thing that we've come up with so far is a drama professor who spent one night in jail for disorderly conduct during a peace demonstration in Kennett Square five years ago."

"Hardly our man," Genelli said.

"I don't know," Meyrowitz said. "If we don't get a good lead soon, maybe we'll have to pin something on this guy." He had his coat and tie off, his shirtsleeves rolled up. His curly hair was wild and damp, and there were dark circles under his eyes.

"How many more from that party to be cleared yet?"

Meyrowitz took his coffee to an uncomfortable tulip-shaped plastic chair beside the desk, sat down. "They've run satisfactory backgrounds on eighty-five of them. There were a hundred and four people at the party. What's that leave? Nineteen to go, right? But you know, somehow I don't think we're going to find a master criminal lurking among them."

They had both spent three hours at the scene in Langhorn, had participated in the initial interrogations of several of the guests at that party across the street from the Recard Institute. And they both knew how clean the theft had been, how untraceable and professional. It was all a dead end out there in Pennsylvania, but every angle of it had to be explored and mapped before it could be written off and forgotten.

"I just talked to Simonsen at the Recard Institute," Genelli said, dropping wearily into the straight-backed chair behind the desk. He sipped his black coffee. "They let the watchman go home at two thirty this afternoon. They've questioned him three times now, a full hour on each occasion. Simonsen swears they've turned his life inside out."

"And?"

"When he was a cop," Genelli said, "he was involved with some underworld figures."

"Rickart was?"

"Yes."

Meyrowitz was interested.

"Don't get your hopes up," Genelli warned. "It was pretty much small time stuff. He took some payoffs in return for leaking word of planned gambling raids . . . It really wasn't worth a trial. He was just quietly retired."

"And went to work at Recard," Meyrowitz said. "When?"

"Eight months ago."

"Are we keeping him under guard?"

"Quiet surveillance," Genelli said. "Four men watching his house. Two men ready to follow his wife and two for him if either of them should try to go anywhere. Two others are tagging after his nineteen-year-old daughter who's supposed to be at a ski lodge over the holiday. There's been a tap on the Rickarts' telephone since four thirty this morning."

"Got the Attorney General out of bed?"

"I suppose." Genelli swigged down some hot coffee and sighed to cool his mouth. "But I don't think John Rickart's past experience with the mob has any tie-in to Robin Hood."

"Probably not," Meyrowitz said. He smiled. "But if we really get in a bind, maybe we can link Rickart to that drama professor who was jailed during the peace march."

Genelli laughed. He finished his coffee and realized that he had drunk it much too fast. He'd have to watch himself, or he'd soon be too jittery to work.

"What now?" Meyrowitz asked.

"While we're waiting for new reports," Genelli said, "let's go over some of the old ones and see if we missed anything."

"We didn't."

"We might have," Genelli insisted. He rummaged through the heaps of files and loose papers on his desk, came up with two folders, the A and B copies of the report on Colonel Theodore Ives. "Let's read this one together. Two minds tackling it at the same time might find something that we overlooked when we went through it separately."

"Ives?" Meyrowitz asked, making an ugly face. "*There's* a stout heart and true if ever I saw one. He *works* at being a patriot, for God's sake!"

"His family might—"

"The boy's an eagle scout. The wife's in the DAR. They spend their weekends together doing family-type things, for God's sake!"

Genelli threw the folder in his lap.

"You're *too* damned thorough," Meyrowitz said. He stared sullenly at the first page of the report.

16.

They had already agreed that Doug would not go to a New York hotel but would stay the night with them. Carrie had engineered it that way so that they could keep both Powell and the tapes in sight. Entering the city by train at six o'clock on New Year's Day, they flagged down a taxi outside of Penn Station and had it take them to the Twentieth Street apartment.

They were all starved. Carrie made a cheese omelet, and they washed the eggs down with a couple of bottles of Great Western Pink Catawba.

"After tomorrow," Doug said, "you won't have to buy cheap wine."

"I've gotten to like it," Lee said.

Carrie said, "Exactly how much money will this Dunio have for us tomorrow night, providing we get the ransom?"

"Not all of it," Powell said. "But the buyer he has lined up for the paintings has already shelled out half a million advance money. Dunio will have that. In cash. He'll deliver the rest of it two weeks from tomorrow."

"Why so long?" Carrie asked.

"First of all, he's got to show the paintings to his buyer and satisfy that man that they're genuine. Then the buyer will put together four and a half million more for us and two and a half million for Dunio."

"What I don't understand," Lee said, pouring another round of wine for everyone, "is why Dunio can't come *here* with the money, like you first said he would."

"It wasn't my idea to change plans," Doug said defensively. "It was Dunio's brainstorm."

Although he strongly suspected that the other man was lying, Lee said, "Yes, I know. But why? Why do we have to drive all the way out to Princeton, New Jersey, to swap the paintings for the first lump of cash?"

Powell shrugged. He was unable to look directly at Lee. "I don't know. I guess Dunio's getting nervous." He drank some wine. "He knows the paintings are stolen. A deal of this size, this importance, he's bound to be on edge. For some reason, he feels more secure at this place in Princeton."

"But is it a secure place for us?" Carrie asked.

"Sure."

Lee tasted his wine. "Is there any chance that Dunio would make a play for the paintings without giving us the money?"

"Absolutely not," Powell said. "He'll bring protection, because he's carrying all that cash. But he'll deal straight with us. For one thing, he'll figure if we could deliver this kind of merchandise once, we could do it again. And he'd want to be the middleman the next time around."

Lee still felt uneasy. He put his hand on Powell's shoulder and waited until the big man raised his head. Lee looked him in the eyes. "I'm putting a lot of faith in you. I'm trusting you."

Powell's long face reflected an inner agony that looked as if it might tear him apart. "I wouldn't let you down. No matter what happens to me, you'll never be touched. I promise." The hard edge of pain in his voice belied the apparent simplicity of his words. What he had said meant more to him than it could to anyone else. Clearly, although the promise had been phrased so tritely, it was a profound commitment in Doug's eyes.

Lee thought of Doug's father. Was that the figure which rose like a specter below the surface meaning of this deeply felt little speech? He was suddenly surprised to see that Powell was on the verge of tears.

"O.K.?" Powell asked.

Lee glanced at Carrie.

She nodded.

"O.K.," Lee said. "We're in this together. I won't doubt you any more. And *I* won't let *you* down, either."

Powell recovered in an instant. Grinning, he picked up his wine glass. "Let's drink to being millionaires!" he said.

17.

New Year's Day—8:00 P.M.

Dropping the venetian slat that he had raised to get a view of Sixty-ninth Street, Gardner Peterson turned away from the window. "You've had an hour to examine the full-depth study of General Powell. If that didn't reveal anything important, then there wasn't anything important to *be* revealed. We don't have a thing to gain by following it up."

"No," Genelli said, from his desk. He knew Peterson was letting politics enter it now. "There are cracks, problems in his family. The kind of problems we've seen linked to less serious security breaks in the past. His wife's the next thing to being a lush. He's apparently alienated his son—"

"Who *isn't* guilty of that kind of failure?" Peterson asked angrily.

"Ives isn't. We've done an exhaustive study of him. His family's straight out of the pages of the *Saturday Evening Post.* But with Powell . . ."

"This is delicate," Peterson said. "We can't question the Chairman of the Joint Chiefs as routinely as we would an ordinary citizen."

"Have the Director finesse him," Genelli said. "I simply *have* to ask him some questions. If I'm right about the leak of the code words, it had to come from Powell or someone close to him. Unless you want to seriously consider the President as a suspect."

Peterson crossed the room to the door, stood there for a moment, thinking about it. "You can interview him on the telephone, can't you?"

"I'm not going to Washington, and I doubt he'll fly here just to satisfy me."

"I'll try to arrange something."

Genelli looked at his watch. "We've only got twenty-one hours until the ransom has to be paid. We've *got* to get a lead!"

New Year's Day—9:30 P.M.

"The Director's called the White House," Peterson said, leaning in the open doorway. "The President's agreed to waive the right of executive privilege. You're free to question Powell."

Genelli raised his eyebrows. "When?"

"Powell will call you from a secure White House line. Probably within the next half hour."

"I can record the conversation?"

"Yes," Peterson said. "But you'll have to type up your own transcript. This can't go by a typist's eyes."

Genelli nodded. "You want to sit in on it?"

"No," Peterson said. "I've got a hundred other things to keep an eye on." That was true. However, Genelli knew that his decision not to participate in the questioning was strictly political. He did not want to share the blame if Genelli ruffled the Chairman of the Joint Chiefs or engendered Presidential wrath.

New Year's Day—11:30 P.M.

Genelli walked down the hall to the unused office at the end where David Meyrowitz was sleeping on a narrow canvas cot. Without turning on the light, he leaned over and shook the young agent by the shoulder.

Meyrowitz sat up, taking a wild punch at the darkness.

"Good thing you aren't wearing your gun," Genelli said. "I'd be full of holes."

"Time's it?"

"Eleven thirty."

Meyrowitz swung his legs off the cot, sat up. "Christ, you let me sleep almost five hours!"

"Shortly," Genelli said, "you'll take over, and I'll get *my* five hours. We've got to be sharp."

The younger man smacked his lips. "God. I feel grimy as a pig."

"Plover drove up from Washington," Genelli said. "Before he left down there, he went to your place and mine, packed suitcases for us. But you can freshen up later. Right now, I have something I want to go over with you."

"Sounds ominous."

"We got the full-depth study on Powell," Genelli said. "It raised a few questions. I pressured Peterson and managed to get a thirty-minute interview with the general."

Meyrowitz got to his feet. "And?"

"Let's go back to my office and discuss it there."

They passed other rooms where lower echelon Bureau field men were shouting into telephones or working busily on reports.

They passed the teletype center where the machines were chattering maniacally, passed Peterson's office where the door was tightly closed.

In the green-walled office, Meyrowitz poured coffee, took his usual chair. He accepted a carbon of the Powell transcript which Genelli had typed himself. The original cartridge of recording tape which contained the entire conversation was locked away in a strongbox in the combination drawer of the desk.

"Pretty long," Meyrowitz said.

"I've circled the salient sections," Genelli said. "Look at page three."

Meyrowitz leafed to the third page and began at the top.

GENELLI: Let me understand this. When you were going to be home for any extended period of time, a full day or more, you put the code book in the safe in your den?

POWELL: That's right.

GENELLI: Haven't you ever worried that the safe might be burglarized?

POWELL: The house has an alarm system. So does the safe. And I rate two personal guards who watch my house when I'm there. A burglar wouldn't get very far, Mr. Genelli.

GENELLI: Well . . . Then who has the combination to the safe, besides you?

POWELL: My wife.

GENELLI: Not your son?

POWELL: No.

GENELLI: You've had the safe for six years, you say. Isn't it possible that your son could have obtained the combination in that time?

POWELL: How could he?

GENELLI: Do you keep the combination written down on a slip of paper in your wallet? Perhaps he saw that. Or perhaps your wife gave it to him.

POWELL: My wife never told him. And my son is not the type to snoop in my wallet. Besides, when would he get the chance?

GENELLI: You have a pool. Do you leave your wallet in the house when you go for a swim?

POWELL: (Pause.) Only my wife and I have that combination.

Meyrowitz looked up from the transcript. "I didn't see the full-depth on Powell. But didn't the preliminary flimsies say that he and his son were at odds?"

Genelli shook his head: yes.

"And here you can feel that," Meyrowitz said, tapping page three of the transcript. "He doesn't want to talk about his son."

Genelli smiled. "See anything else of interest?"

Meyrowitz sipped his coffee. "Despite what the general says, he just doesn't trust his boy. He never gave him the combination."

Genelli nodded. He said, "Page five, about halfway down from the top, then on to page six."

Meyrowitz found the marked passage.

GENELLI: Now, sir, this may seem like an extremely personal question. But I've been authorized to ask you anything. I'm afraid I'll have to pry a bit into sensitive areas.

POWELL: Don't worry about that. Go ahead.

GENELLI: Our detailed file on your family indicates that Mrs. Powell is a heavy social drinker. On several public occasions, having drunk too much, she has been less than discreet in discussing her own, your, and even the President's opinions of various reporters, Congressmen, and other Washington figures.

POWELL: (Silence.)

GENELLI: The Bureau has found that a history of minor indiscretions can lead to a more major security problem. Now . . . Only you are in the position to know if your wife is more than a problem drinker. Is she now an alcoholic?

POWELL: (Silence.)

GENELLI: Forgive me. It's a necessary question.

POWELL: (Silence for several seconds.) Very well. She *has* taken to drinking alone. It isn't just social drinking anymore. But the notion that Loretta would want to—or even know *how* to get mixed up in something like this theft . . . It's ludicrous.

GENELLI: Most likely, you're right, General.

"You better solve this thing," Meyrowitz said, smiling ruefully. "Because only success is going to justify those questions."

"Page eight," Genelli said.

POWELL: What father *is* close to his son these days?

GENELLI: Then there's considerable distance between the two of you?

POWELL: Miles. But we're on speaking terms, at least. And he's slowly coming out of this awful mood he's been in. He'll be all right.

GENELLI: Is this break with your son recent? And what caused it?

POWELL: He expected me to use my rank to pull a soft assignment for him when he was drafted. But I did just the opposite. I made sure he got the kind of hardening he needed. He spent a year in Vietnam, pretty much because I pulled strings to get him sent there. He resents that. But I think he's slowly coming to understand that it was good for him.

GENELLI: You do? Why?

POWELL: Oh, for one thing . . . I have a large military library in my den at home, and there's a section that contains almost every book ever written about Vietnam, both liberal and conservative. He's been spending a lot of time in there, recently. He's been looking over those books, doing some studying. He told me he's beginning to change his mind on some things about the war.

"Spending lots of time in the den?" Meyrowitz asked, looking up from the transcript.

Genelli sighed, nodded.

"The same den that has the safe? The safe to which this kid has no combination?"

Genelli laced his knuckles, cracked them. "Page fourteen."

> GENELLI: Have you ever discussed the existence of the code book with either your wife or son?
>
> POWELL: They know about it.
>
> GENELLI: But have you ever specifically discussed it with them, in detail?
>
> POWELL: I suppose. After all, a man likes to talk to his family about his work. And look here, there's nothing particularly secret about the mere *existence* of the code book.

"I think maybe you have something," Meyrowitz said.

Genelli searched for, found, and passed over a sheet of yellow paper which had been torn from the full-depth report on General Norman Powell and his family. "You've seen only the preliminary flimsies on the Powells. This is from the full-depth. It's a paragraph on his son's college experiences."

Meyrowitz read it. His dark face brightened.

"Interesting?"

"He studied computer science twice," Meyrowitz said. "Once, before he was drafted, at MIT. After his discharge—at Recard?" He looked up. "What are you waiting for?"

"Your opinion."

"Put out a pick-up order on Douglas Eugene Powell," Meyrowitz said.

Genelli was pleased to have the younger man's support, although he would have gone ahead without it. "I've already drafted a request for a warrant. I've given it to Peterson. I'm only waiting for his O.K." Genelli picked up his copy of the transcript of the Powell interview. "Just one more thing that I want you to read. Page seventeen."

Meyrowitz studied the marked passage.

GENELLI: Sir, do you recall if you might ever have mentioned to either your son or your wife that yours was one of only three code books which was complete, which contained all fifty of the primary code words?

POWELL: I might have.

GENELLI: I'd like you to be more definite about this, if you can. (Pause of five seconds.)

POWELL: Well, I'm not any different from anyone else; I'm only human. I think most men would tend to brag to their families about a thing of this sort. After all, it's an honor; it's quite a—status symbol.

GENELLI: Then you talked to your wife and son about this aspect of the code book?

POWELL: I probably said something to the effect that my security clearance was one of the highest three in the country. I probably told them how special the code book was.

Meyrowitz scratched his head, stared at the paper and then at his superior. "I give up. What's so damned important about this exchange?"

Genelli held up one hand in a V for victory sign. "Let's make two suppositions. One, that Douglas Powell is our man. Two, that he knows that his father's code book is one of only three which contain all fifty code words." He lowered his hand. "When he went into that computer room in the Recard Institute, Douglas Powell knew that by stealing a wide variety of data he was limiting our investigation to three men and their families: the President, Colonel Ives, and his own father. He was setting himself up to be caught."

"Jesus!" Meyrowitz said.

Genelli got to his feet, too nervous to sit still any longer. "If Douglas Powell would jeopardize his own future, risk twenty or more years in jail, *want* to get caught—whether to strike out at his father, to make a name for himself as a revolutionary, or for whatever reasons—wouldn't he be perfectly capable of passing those tapes to the Chinese or the Russians? Wouldn't he be capable of *anything?*"

18.

January 2—12:30 A.M.

Sitting behind the wheel of the unmarked Bureau sedan across the street from Ilya Zaitsev's apartment building, Agent Packer munched on a cheeseburger and sipped cola from a plastic cup. "Since you been on this kind of duty, you ever had an alert like this one?" he asked Ashe.

"Once," Ashe said, around a mouthful of french fries. "Some Air Force captain walked off with a folder of fighter plane specifications. The CIA had been expecting him to do something like that, so we had a tail on him. He spotted the tail and lost him fast. Everyone panicked. Because we didn't have the slightest idea who his contact was, we sharpened our surveillance on every foreign national in the New York-Washington area."

"You think it's something like that this time?" Packer asked.

"Sure," Ashe said. "Everyone's panicked. Someone's probably walked away with the Pentagon's purchase order for washroom supplies." Ashe was upset by the change in his nightly routine which the alert had caused. He liked to eat his late-night meal in a restaurant while his partner handled the stake-out by himself. No one should have to eat dinner cooped up in a car.

"Well," Packer said, finishing his sandwich, "maybe it's a good thing. Maybe there'll be some excitement around here for a change."

"Excitement, I can do without," Ashe said.

January 2—6:00 A.M.

When Genelli came back to his office after his five-hour nap, he found Meyrowitz sitting at his desk. Genelli had left the stacks of files and messages arranged rather neatly; now, thanks to Meyrowitz, they were a scattered, rumpled mess. Papers had fallen to the floor on all sides and teetered in a heap on the spare office chair. Oblivious of the chaotic conditions around him, Meyrowitz was busily working on an assignments chart for some aspect of the investigation.

"You look right at home there," Genelli said. "I never thought you were ambitious, but now I see you *do* have a lean and hungry look."

"That comes from drinking four gallons of coffee and eating only one ham-and-cheese and one pastry in twenty-four hours." He stood up and tacked the new assignments chart to the wall. Turning back to Genelli, who had made straight for the coffee machine, he said, "How'd you sleep?"

"Like a stone."

"Good," Meyrowitz said. "Because they way things are going, that'll be the last sleep you'll get this month."

"What's wrong?"

Meyrowitz rubbed his bloodshot eyes with the backs of his

hands. He sighed loudly. "Two hours ago, Peterson came in to say there isn't enough evidence against Douglas Powell to justify an arrest warrant."

"God damn!"

"My sentiments exactly," Meyrowitz agreed. "I argued with him. I said, sure the evidence is circumstantial. But in this situation, it's well worth risking a warrant on it. Peterson said, sure enough it *was* worth risking a warrant on it—for anyone except the son of the Chairman of the Joint Chiefs."

"Politics," Genelli said angrily. That was one thing that had not gotten in his way on the Zilinski-Ross case. Neither of those maniacs had had an influential father. "Why didn't you wake me as soon as you heard Peterson's decision?"

"You needed your sleep," Meyrowitz said. "Besides, what could you have done? Spit, scream, and thump your head against the wall? Anyway, Peterson's compromising. We're using forty agents to learn everything we can about Douglas Powell—including where he is right now."

Genelli walked over to the desk and looked at the jumble of files and reports. "That's in the transcript of my conversation with the general. The boy's supposed to be spending this week at some hotel down in Miami."

"We've looked into that."

"And he isn't there, of course."

"It was the Hotel Doral, according to the general. But the boy never made reservations there," Meyrowitz said. "And he's not at any of three dozen other big hotels down there."

"Peterson knows all this?"

"Yes."

Genelli's dark eyes narrowed. "And he still won't go to a judge for an arrest warrant?"

"No."

"Shit!" Genelli said. He almost threw his cupful of hot coffee at the wall.

"I've made an assignments chart of the agents who're trying to get a lead on the kid," Meyrowitz said, pointing to the legal-size sheet of paper he had just tacked up. "With any luck at all, if we keep a full forty men moving on this, we'll discover where he's gone."

"They're looking into his associates and friends?" Genelli asked.

"Sure. But he's a loner. Doesn't seem to have many friends."

"Any that look like potential partners?" Genelli asked, realizing that he was no longer even supposing Douglas Powell's guilt.

"None that are obvious," Meyrowitz said. "We're checking on them, but all his friends seem like nice ordinary people."

"Until a few hours ago," Genelli said, "so did he."

January 2—7:00 A.M.

At the kitchen table Doug Powell used a dozen rags which Carrie had given him to fill the empty spaces between the magnetic tapes packed into his largest suitcase. He closed the bag, used a key to lock it. Sliding it off the table, he tested its weight. "I can manage it."

Carrie, who was sitting across the table from him, frowned at the suitcase. "I'm still not sure I understand why it's necessary to move them out of here."

Powell was still angry with Lee for having brought her into the operation. She was too damned aggressive, not at all the kind of woman he appreciated. But he knew that she was the key to keeping Lee's confidence, and he tried to give her a reasonable answer. "For one thing, once we've got the ransom and are ready to mail the tapes back to the Pentagon, it'll confuse the issue if we send them from Princeton instead of New York." That sounded too weak to be convincing, and he decided to give her some of the truth. "I've told you I'm going to be a suspect. That can't be avoided. The FBI's going to be investigating me and my friends. I wouldn't even be surprised if a couple of them visited you today. If they do show up, and if they go so far as to run a search of this apartment . . . Well, you sure don't want to have those tapes in the closet."

Lee was leaning against the refrigerator, drinking a glass of milk. "Surely they wouldn't search your friends' homes unless they were damned certain it was you they were after. You're talking as if you're bound to get nailed for this."

Be careful, Powell told himself. When you lied as much as he had been forced to lie to Lee, you could easily trip yourself up in your own deceptions. "I'm ninety-nine per cent sure I'll come out of this. But if they *do* get me for it, I can let Doug Powell die and be Dan Walters for the rest of my life. I can waltz right out of the country with my share of the money. But you can't. You're the ones who have to be kept perfectly clean."

Powell saw the two of them exchange a quick glance.

Lee finished his milk. "I guess you're right."

"Of course."

"But be careful with those tapes," Lee said.

Laughing, Powell picked up the heavy suitcase and then the one that contained his clothes. "I'm not likely to lose them."

"You want me to help you carry one of those downstairs?" Lee asked.

"No," Powell said. "They're really not that heavy." He took a deep breath, winked at them. "Good luck with the subway business."

"It'll go like clockwork," Lee said.

"I'll see you in Princeton later tonight. You still have the map I drew?"

"We've got it," Carrie said.

He did not like the searching way she stared at him.

Powell left the apartment. On Twentieth Street, he walked two blocks to Sixth Avenue and caught a cab going uptown.

At the Port Authority bus terminal, he checked his bags into two rental lockers. He had a quick breakfast of toast and eggs at a coffee shop, then retrieved his bags and went outside and hailed another taxi.

This time, he went to La Guardia Airport. He could have taken the first cab there. This switch was a precaution against the FBI or anyone else ever being able to trace him from La Guardia back to within a couple of blocks of Lee's place.

He had made a promise which he meant to keep. Whether or not he himself escaped, Lee Ackridge would never be linked to the theft.

At La Guardia, using his Dan Walters identification, he rented a car from Avis. Eventually, the FBI was going to tumble to his use of the Walters name and sniff out this rental. But not just yet. Not, in fact, until and if they interrogated Pia James.

When the car was brought around to him, he put the heaviest suitcase behind the driver's seat. He put the other one beside him on the front seat, because it contained the two Colt Diamondback .38 Specials. Both guns were loaded.

He drove back into the city, across midtown Manhattan and, against the flow of rush hour traffic, out through the Lincoln Tunnel. On the other side of the Hudson, he took the New Jersey Turnpike south towards Princeton.

He kept looking in the rear-view mirror, even though he knew that they could not have located him and put a tail on him already. By now, the FBI would have narrowed down its investigation to one of those three complete code books: his father's. They would have checked the Doral Hotel in Miami Beach and would know that he had never shown up there. Because the ransom was to be paid in New York City, they would have begun a frantic search for him in Manhattan. But he was now on his way to Princeton . . .

Although he could sometimes blind himself to truths which he did not want to face, by this time the general must have finally admitted that his son was the data thief. What was the old bastard doing this very minute? Indulging in one of his screaming fits? And what of sweet Loretta? Chugging away at gin-and-tonic even though it was hours until lunchtime?

Rushing southward across the industrial wastelands of northern New Jersey, Douglas Powell grinned humorlessly.

January 2—10:10 A.M.

As soon as he opened the door, Lee knew who they were. One of them was six-two and weighed two-twenty; although there was something hard about him, he was clean-cut, watchful, and obviously intelligent. The other man was two inches shorter and thirty pounds lighter, but he was otherwise a twin to the first. They were both dressed in conservative gray suits; one wore a black overcoat. The other preferred blue.

"Yes?" he asked.

"Mr. Ackridge?" the bigger man asked. "Lee Ackridge?"

"That's me. What can I do for you?"

"FBI, Mr. Ackridge," the smaller man said. They both presented badges and cards.

"For God's sake!" Lee said, wondering if he were reacting as an innocent, bewildered man would have done.

"We'd like to ask you some questions," the smaller man said.

According to the ID he had shown, his name was Ogilvey.

"May we come in?" the taller one asked. His name was Keyes.

Lee showed them to the couch in the living room and sat across from them in a tattered old maroon easy chair. "What's this all about?"

The two agents looked the room over from where they sat. Then they stared at Lee for a moment as if he were just another piece of the shabby furniture. Keyes, the big man, finally said, "Do you know a man named Douglas Eugene Powell?"

"Doug? Hell, of course. We were in the war together. We—" He stopped himself, let his expression change. He slid forward anxiously on his chair. "Hey, has something happened to Doug?"

"Not exactly," Keyes said.

Ogilvey said, "When was the last time you saw Mr. Powell?"

Lee thought a moment. "Just before Christmas of last year."

"A week ago?" Ogilvey asked.

"No, no. I meant two Christmases back. Better than a year ago."

The two agents looked at each other.

Was that disappointment in their faces? Had they accepted the lie so quickly?

"You still haven't told me what's happened to Doug," Lee said, a false note of concern in his voice.

They both ignored the question.

Keyes said, "Mr. Ackridge, would you mind if we looked around your apartment?"

Although he had been expecting the request, Lee tried to seem surprised by it. "What for?"

"To see if Mr. Powell is here."

"But I've told you—"

Ogilvey, who had a sharper tongue than Keyes, said, "We can put this place under guard and go get a search warrant if you want to force the issue."

"But," said Keyes, tempering his partner's acid approach, "we'd sure appreciate it if you gave us permission."

"Wait a minute," Lee said, suspicion entering his voice. "It's not what I thought it was at first. Nothing's happened to Doug. He's done something, and now you're after him."

Ogilvey said nothing.

Keyes merely nodded.

"What's he done?" Lee asked.

"We aren't at liberty to say," Keyes told him.

Lee shook his head, amazed. "Good God, do you know who his father is? Well, of course you do." He stood up. "Look, Doug and I went through a hell of a lot together. But even the kind of friendship that comes out of a war has its limits. I wouldn't set myself up as an accessory to a crime. I *am* studying law. I know what kind of mess I could get into. Come on. I'll show you around the other rooms."

They rummaged in closets and checked under the bed. They did not restrict their search to those places large enough to hide a man; instead, they poked around wherever there was sufficient space to conceal six large reels of magnetic computer tape.

Half an hour after they had begun the search, they returned to the living room and sat down again.

"I'm sorry we had to inconvenience you," Keyes said apologetically. "Could we impose on you for another half hour? We have a good many questions we'd like to ask.

"By all means," Lee said. "I'll do what I can to help."

19.

January 2—1:00 P.M.

With only four hours remaining until the scheduled ransom drop, Roy Genelli dismissed Agents Keyes and Ogilvey and leaned back in his chair trying to figure where in the hell their information left him. He was still balancing on two legs of his chair, his feet hooked on the horizontal brace under the desk, when Gardner Peterson entered the room.

"Everything's coming up empty on my end," the supervisor said. "Anything new on your angle?"

Although he had slept no more than anyone else, Peterson looked quite as neat and composed as he had at the start of all this, in that Pentagon office thirty-four hours ago. His white hair was neatly combed. He had apparently just used one of the showers and had slipped into a freshly pressed suit.

"We're making headway," Genelli said. "But not fast enough."

David Meyrowitz was standing by the assignments chart using

a felt-tip pen to X out the names of two of the few remaining agents who were following up possible leads on Douglas Powell and his friends. He turned to Peterson and said, "If the President could officially turn the clock back twelve hours, we'd have time enough to wrap this thing up."

Peterson sat down. "Then you're getting closer?"

"I exaggerated," Meyrowitz admitted. "Given an extra twelve hours, we could tell beyond doubt who Powell's accomplice was and precisely how the two of them pulled off the theft. But even then, we couldn't get our hands on them."

"Are you purposefully talking riddles?" Peterson asked.

Rocking back and forth on two legs of his chair, Genelli closed his eyes and tried to order his thoughts. "We're sure Powell's the one, but he must have accomplices."

Meyrowitz finished drawing a last X on the chart. "Barring any major gap in our knowledge of his associates," Meyrowitz said, "we've boiled it down to two candidates." He crossed to the corner table to cut himself a wedge of cheese cake which had been ordered up at lunchtime.

"The first suspect," Genelli said, his eyes still closed, "is one Lee Frederick Ackridge, who was supposedly at home with his girlfriend, just the two of them, on New Year's Eve. Ackridge was in Powell's unit in Vietnam, and they were very close friends over there. A couple of months before his tour of duty was up, Ackridge was badly hurt in action and sent home early. Facial burns. He's had plastic surgery, but remains scarred."

"He's got a grudge then," Peterson said. "A motive."

Swallowing a mouthful of cheese cake, Meyrowitz said, "He sure looked like our man. He's here in New York. And after what he went through in the war, he might think this kind of risk was well worth taking."

"I sent Keyes and Ogilvey to Ackridge's apartment building," Genelli said. "They got there at seven thirty this morning, questioned the neighbors. Those who know Ackridge and this Carrie Hoffman who lives with him think he's nice and she's a genuine angel."

"The old woman who lives across the hall from them denounced the FBI for even *suspecting* Carrie of the slightest misbehavior," Meyrowitz said.

"Ackridge could be involved without this girl's knowledge," Peterson said.

"That's what Keyes and Ogilvey thought," Genelli said. "They didn't get to see her right away, because she was at work by the time they finished with the neighbors. Anyway, they talked to Ackridge. And they searched his apartment with his permission. No rubber masks, burglar's tools, or magnetic tapes. The only thing . . . In a closet, Keyes saw a coat somewhat like the one Rickart described. But it wasn't an exact match."

"Rickart could have given an inaccurate description," Peterson said.

"Except," Meyrowitz said, "there must be a million heavy, navy blue, mid-thigh coats in New York. I'd be surprised if Ackridge *didn't* have one."

Genelli pushed his chair back, got to his feet, and began to pace as he talked. "He was entirely cooperative. Keyes observed that, with one half of Ackridge's face paralyzed, it was difficult to judge his expressions, his reactions to important questions. But he thinks that Ackridge was really bewildered by the whole thing."

"Still no reason to drop him from the suspect list," Peterson said. He got to his feet, because he was uncomfortable when Genelli could look down on him.

"Well," Genelli said, "when I sent Keyes and Ogilvey to see Ackridge, I sent two more men to interview Ackridge's psychiatrist, Dr. Leon Slatvik. He has offices on Park Avenue. The government's been paying him to treat Ackridge for extreme depression and psychosomatic impotency."

Peterson had been pacing away from Genelli. He turned on his heel and said, "Impotency? But you said he was living with a woman."

"Apparently," Genelli said, "she's every bit as extraordinary as her neighbors say she is."

"I'm surprised Dr. Slatvik would give you such personal information. There *is* a legal secrecy between doctor and patient."

"We didn't get that from Slatvik," Genelli said. "We found it in Veteran's Administration files. Slatvik didn't want to talk about Ackridge until he discovered we knew the man's condition. Then he was willing to answer certain questions. The nut of it is —he said Ackridge would not, at this point in his recovery, be able to take the sort of initiative we suspected him of taking. According to Slatvik, Ackridge could not have conquered his inferiority complex long enough to participate in a dangerous and clever crime unless Miss Hoffman urged him to it."

"And he thinks Carrie Hoffman is an angel on earth," Meyrowitz said. "According to Slatvik, she's Ackridge's only hope."

"Has anyone obtained a first-hand evaluation of this woman?"

"When they were finished with Ackridge," Genelli said, "Keyes and Ogilvey went to the offices where she works. They questioned her for half an hour."

"And?"

Genelli smiled. "Keyes says she has the most beautiful smile and the most perfect complexion he's ever seen."

Meyrowitz chimed in: "And Ogilvey could love her for her blue eyes alone."

"But you're still keeping them under full surveillance?"

Genelli nodded. "Two men watching their apartment house entrance, two more in the alley behind. We've got men watching her office building. Neither of them can go anywhere without a tail."

"Who's the other suspect?" Peterson asked.

Genelli went and got a cup of coffee. "The other man is Howard Dunio. He was a sergeant in Powell's unit in Vietnam. After Ackridge was sent home, Dunio was Powell's closest friend over there. Although it's never been able to get proof, the Army's sure Dunio was involved in smuggling artifacts out of Southeast Asia. He left the service two years ago, and since then he's become a wanted man in Laos and in Thailand. Both countries are after him for smuggling out nationally protected antique art."

"He's also wanted for questioning in England, France, Denmark, Belgium, and Italy," Meyrowitz said. "In every case it has to do with the sale of stolen paintings."

Peterson was suddenly more animated than he had been all morning. "If Powell *is* behind this, and if Dunio's his partner, that would explain the ransom demand. If Dunio deals in stolen art, he'd know how to fence these paintings they've asked for!"

"But if we accept the obvious—that Powell and Dunio are Robin Hood—we're stalled," Genelli said.

"Stalled? Why?"

"We've tapped Interpol files," Genelli said, folding his hands around the cup of coffee, letting it warm him. "That takes time, and we've gotten very little from them so far. But what we have learned is disheartening. Dunio has disappeared."

Massaging the back of his neck with one hand, Peterson said, "I don't understand."

"A man answering Dunio's description has been operating in the international hot art market for two years, using as many as nine different names. He must have full documentation for each of his identities, all of it forged, because Interpol has been unable to pinpoint his home base. He changes names and nationalities like a chameleon changes colors. He's probably living somewhere in Europe or the United States, using a false name which he reserves strictly for his private life."

"We have more resources than Interpol," Peterson said. "If

we throw ourselves into it, get the CIA on his trail, we can find—"

"I doubt it," Genelli interrupted. "Naturally, we've got to bust ass trying. But . . . If a man is wanted by the law under his own name, and if he has access to perfectly forged papers, he has the motivation and the means to begin a whole new life. He has to be willing to make a clean break with the past, of course. He can never see his relatives and old friends again, and he must stay away from his old haunts, favorite restaurants, theaters . . . Most men who try to establish a new identity can't make a clean enough break with the past. Sentiment and habit undo them. But from what we've gotten out of Interpol and our own files, it looks to me as if Dunio is the kind of man who's tough enough to sacrifice his past without a second thought."

"You see, I wasn't talking in riddles," Meyrowitz said, sitting in the third chair. "We're pretty sure who we're after—but we don't have much hope of nabbing them at this point."

Peterson got to his feet. "I'll have an arrest warrant for Dunio within the hour. We'll have to manufacture files on a couple of fake agents and accuse Dunio of killing them. If we had to put the word 'treason' on the warrant, we'd blow this thing apart."

"You'll want to put tails on Dunio's relatives and old friends," Genelli said. "I can't see him breaking cover like that—but he might."

"What about a warrant for Powell on suspicion?" Meyrowitz asked.

Peterson grimaced. "Politics. We'll probably get it, but I have to go through the Director for that one."

"And he'll have to go through the President," Meyrowitz said.

Peterson shrugged.

"Every minute counts," Genelli said.

"I'm sure the Director understands," Peterson said.

"If worse comes to worst," Genelli said, "we can still hope to nail them during the ransom drop."

"We'll have three hundred men in Manhattan by five o'clock," Peterson said. "Every one of them will have seen photographs of Dunio and Powell. If we concentrate our forces around the ransom drop and at all possible exits from the subway system, we can't miss. We'll get them." He knew he could not convince Genelli. He was only talking to reassure himself.

"What about the ransom?" Genelli asked.

"I'm to pick up the paintings at two o'clock and bring them back here." He looked at his watch and stood up. "I'd better be going. I should be back by three." At the doorway, he turned to Genelli again. "God knows what we've promised the Nationalist Chinese in return for these paintings. Military support? Trade agreements?" The blood drained out of his face as he thought of it. "We better not let these people get away. We better nail them in that subway train, or we'll be standing in shit up to our necks." He looked at his watch again, turned, and left.

"You see that ax hanging up there now?" Meyrowitz asked.

20.

January 2—3:15 P.M.

Five miniature paintings, each measuring approximately seven by eleven inches including the permanent mounting, were carefully arranged on the desk in Gardner Peterson's office. They were exquisite watercolors rendered on silk, and Roy Genelli thought they were among the most striking works of art he had ever seen. These colorful, flat surfaces seemed to do more than reflect the light; instead, they absorbed it and altered it and gave back these unearthly visions and rich but delicate hues. All five were inhumanly beautiful Chinese landscapes containing no trace of man in their depictions of an ethereal and fragile Nature.

"The top three," Peterson said, "were painted by Ku K'ai Chih in the fourth century, after but still in the influence of the Han Dynasty. The other two are the work of an artist to whom the Sung Dynasty acted as a patron in the tenth century. That was the Periclean age of Chinese art."

"You sound like an expert," Meyrowitz said.

"It's information from the Nationalist Chinese curator," Peterson explained. "I believe he was actually sick to his stomach at the thought of turning them over to me. He kept trying to delay it."

These five paintings, Genelli knew, had been on display at the Metropolitan Museum and were part of an exhibit of sixty-two pieces of Chinese art. They were on loan not from mainland China but from the government of Formosa, which had also dispatched a curator to watch over them while they were in the United States. And now that same curator had been forced, by an order from his own government, to relinquish the five most prized pieces of that exhibit.

"Any idea how much these would bring on the international black market?" Meyrowitz asked.

"They're priceless," Peterson said. "It's as if Michelangelo's statue of David was put up for sale. What do you think that would bring? A million? Two million? Ten? Well, this is the Eastern equivalent of that kind of sale."

"It's criminal to use these as ransom, to let them fall into the hands of a man like Dunio," Genelli said.

Peterson's reply was quick and sharp. "You *won't* let them fall into anyone's hands. You'll catch Dunio—or whoever's behind this—when he picks up the paintings on that subway train."

"Let's face facts," Meyrowitz said, ignoring Peterson's scowl. "We're going to *try* to at least put a tail on one of them during the ransom pickup. But we could fail. They might have something clever arranged; after all, they've been damned clever up until now. That's why we're bugging both the paintings and the box they'll be packed in; because if we lose him on the train, we can follow him electronically the moment he comes up into the streets again."

Peterson glared at him. When Meyrowitz just stared placidly

back at him, the supervisor looked down at the paintings and calmed himself. "At least these won't be scattered all over the world in the private collections of rich men. Chances are a thousand to one that they'll be offered to Peking, and they'll end up in a museum there. That's where Chiang Kai-shek got them when the Kuomintang fell apart in 1949."

"Well," said Meyrowitz brightly, "it's nice to see that justice always triumphs in the end."

"That isn't funny," Peterson said.

21.

January 2—3:30 P.M.

Feeling slightly foolish, Lee Ackridge put on the long-haired brown wig which Carrie had bought for him last week. He worked with it until it seemed perfectly natural. Staring critically at his reflection in the bathroom mirror, he saw that he had been transformed from a straight, sober-looking student lawyer into a long-haired kid. Next, he used theatrical makeup to cover the worst of the scars on his temple and cheek. When he shrugged into a topcoat and wound a scarf around his scarred neck, he did not look like himself.

That was the idea.

He turned off the bathroom light and went into the bedroom. There, he set the automatic light timer—one of three which Carrie had bought last week—so that the bedside lamp would switch on at four o'clock, then off again at a quarter to six. In the kitchen, he set the timer to turn on the overhead light at five o'clock. He turned on the living room light and set the timer to switch it off a few minutes before five, then on again at six. To anyone watching the building from Twentieth Street, the action with the lights over the next couple of hours would seem to prove that he was home and moving about.

That was the idea.

He went to the door, opened it a crack, and saw the third floor hall was empty. He stepped outside, quickly locked the door, and went downstairs. He did not leave the building, but continued down to the basement.

In the 1930s, a real estate development company had constructed three apartment houses here, all with shared walls. Over the years, the project had deteriorated and changed hands more than once. However, because the parcel had never been split, no one had ever sealed off the basement connections between the three buildings. In the cellar, Lee found the door to the second apartment house, crossed that basement, and entered the basement of the third and final building.

It was here that the superintendent for all three houses lived, but at the moment he was nowhere in evidence. Lee found the stairs and went cautiously up to the main floor.

Still no one.

The building was quiet.

At the street door, he hesitated only an instant, then went out into the cold January afternoon. Already, day was waning. He walked up toward Sixth Avenue, past a dark car where two men sat watching *another* building.

He expected to be stopped even though he was disguised and even though he had come out of an apartment house two doors down from the one that they had been watching. But no one cried out.

He turned the corner and kept walking. He had gotten away with it.

JANUARY 2, 4:30 P.M.–9:00 P.M.

The Ransom

22.

January 2—4:30 P.M.

A substantial part of the special FBI force that had been established in Manhattan to cover the ransom pickup was concentrated in mobile units. Peterson had requisitioned forty-six unmarked Bureau cars. Each sedan carried its driver and two riders; each man carried a revolver and had access to the shotgun clamped on the back of the front seat. All forty-six teams were in position by 4:30 P.M., thirty-five minutes before the operation was scheduled to get underway.

At the intersection of Fourteenth Street and Seventh Avenue, above the subway station where David Meyrowitz would board the rush-hour express train with the paintings under his arm, there were three Bureau cars. One of them faced west on Fourteenth, another faced east, and the third car was parked between Fourteenth and Thirteenth, facing into Seventh Avenue South. They all had their engines running and their two-way radios turned to a static-filled but otherwise silent channel.

The next group of cars was clustered in the vicinity of Penn Station, which would be the train's first stop after Fourteenth Street and one of the two most likely places for Robin Hood to debark with the ransom. One unit was parked between Thirty-third and Thirty-fourth, aimed south along Seventh Avenue. The other cars were on Eighth Avenue, Thirty-first, and Thirty-fourth: five of them altogether.

In Times Square, the train's second stop, there were six cars arranged on Forty-second, Forty-third, Broadway, and Seventh Avenue. Because he felt that the confusion of Times Square at rush hour would most appeal to Robin Hood as the place to come off the subway, Roy Genelli was one of the three men in the cruiser parked opposite the Rialto Theater on Forty-second Street, facing east toward Broadway.

Four cruisers were positioned in the streets above the train's third stop at Seventy-second and Broadway, and four more at the stop after that one up on Ninety-sixth and Broadway.

Those positions alone used up twenty-two of their mobile units. They counted themselves lucky that Robin Hood had not chosen a local for the ransom drop.

The remaining twenty-four mobile units were covering all of the most accessible exits from Manhattan: the George Washington Bridge, the Lincoln and Holland Tunnels, the Brooklyn-Battery Tunnel, the Brooklyn Bridge, the Manhattan and Williamsburg Bridges, the Queens-Midtown Tunnel, and the Queensboro Bridge. It had even been necessary to put four cars on the F.D.R. Drive north of Gracie Mansion, in order to be able to intercept any suspect vehicle before it could reach one of the bridges over the Harlem River.

In addition to the 138 men on wheels, another 125 agents were patrolling on foot in and around those stations where the train would make its scheduled stops. It was possible that Robin Hood would try to leave one train for another, and there had to be enough agents to pick up on a change like that.

Working in the Bureau offices on Sixty-ninth Street, another thirty-seven agents attempted to monitor the mobile units and maintain a running account of all other aspects of the operation.

Four men were watching the Ackridge-Hoffman apartment, and four others were maintaining surveillance on the exits to the office building where Carrie Hoffman worked.

Three hundred and eight FBI agents.

Six civilian secretaries.

One FBI district supervisor.

Only a handful of them were aware of the circumstances behind this desperately important operation, but all of them were impatiently counting the minutes until 5:05 P.M.

23.

January 2—4:35 P.M.

Pia James parked her Mercedes on Twenty-fifth Street between Seventh and Eighth Avenues and left it unlocked as she had been told to do. She walked out to Seventh and turned south toward Fourteenth Street.

The wind was not as bad as it could often be at this time of year in New York. But there was a strong breeze, and the temperature was hovering around fifteen degrees. By the time she had gone two blocks, her nose was cold, her cheeks flushed. In three blocks, her ears were ringing and numb. The breeze *felt* like a wind by the time she reached Nineteenth Street; it cut through her Beged-Or coat and chilled her breasts.

This was ridiculous. She was going to catch pneumonia. And was that worth five thousand dollars?

Hell, yes! Five thousand dollars was two weeks' earnings. And she could make it in just a couple of hours, without letting anyone use her body. It was worth an eleven-block walk and a little subway ride.

It wasn't worth jail, though.

But she would keep her eyes open. If at any point she sensed cops moving in, she'd drop the damned box and to hell with Dan Walters or whoever he was.

Walking briskly, she reached the Fourteenth Street station a couple of minutes before five o'clock. As she went down the steps, she realized with something of a shock that the man ahead of her was the contact. He was carrying a foot-square box wrapped in plain brown paper and tied around with binder twine, decorated with a rectangular red shipping tag. It was the package for which Walters had told her to watch. However, the man carrying it was not what she had expected. He was five-ten, with dark curly hair and a dusty complexion that made him look like an Arab. He was not the least bit like a hood; instead, he was cute and kind of sexy.

Pia James stayed well behind him and kept out of his line of sight. Even if he saw her, he would not know it was she who would eventually possess that box. Nevertheless, she tried to keep out of his way: no sense in him being able to identify her if *he* was busted.

The minutes crawled along.

Madelaine Harlow, as she had started calling herself when she came to the city four years ago, got out of the taxi at Seventh Avenue and Seventeenth Street. She stood on the curb until the cab disappeared around the corner and the driver could no longer see her. Then she walked south toward Fourteenth Street.

She wore a long gray wool sweater-dress and a black jacket with fur lining, a Bergdorf Goodman ensemble. She was overdressed for the neighborhood. And she was dangerously pretty for the neighborhood as well: tall, leggy, with ash-blond hair and big green eyes. She wasn't the least bit worried about crime in the streets, though. She had walked the streets for a full year before she managed to set herself up with a residential clientele, and she knew how to handle herself.

The only thing that bothered her was the shopping bag she had to carry. For one thing, it was from Korvettes. And she *never* bought anything at Korvettes. For another thing, although the bag looked as if it were full of purchases, it was only puffed up with lightly rumpled toilet paper. Madelaine felt rather silly walking down the street with a bag full of toilet paper, pretending it was a bit heavy when it really weighed only a few ounces.

She reached the steps of the Fourteenth Street subway station at one minute before five o'clock. Downstairs, only sixty or seventy people were gathered on her side of the platform, and only thirty of them were standing around the pillar where she had been told to wait. She walked over and stood with them.

A curly-headed man in his late twenties gave her a careful, appreciative look. She returned his admiration with a cool, superior smirk. He was handsome, but obviously not rich. Madelaine liked men who were rich, or getting there.

In a year or two, when she had more experience, a better apartment, and a wardrobe of the right quality, she would maybe be as good, as high-priced, and as successful a call girl as Pia James already was. That was her ambition, anyway.

January 2—5:00 P.M.

David Meyrowitz had entered the station shortly before five o'clock and had posted himself by the pillar that had been described in the teletyped ransom demand that the thieves had sent from Langhorn a day and a half ago. Nothing about it made it any different from the dozens of other pillars supporting the street above—except for the white letters which had been hastily spray-painted on all four sides: RH, RH, RH, RH.

Occasionally, he surveyed the growing crowd around him, but he did not dare stare too long at anyone. Robin Hood was not likely to be the shy type; but he certainly didn't want to scare off the bastard.

Meyrowitz was worried by Dunio's and Powell's absence from the crowd. It just wasn't possible that one of them could have boarded the train farther down the line with any *absolute* certainty that his car would stop in front of the marked pillar and open to admit the ransom bearer. Robin Hood had to be getting on at this station. Which meant there was a third party besides Powell and Dunio.

Don't stare.

Don't blow it.

Moments later the train screamed out of the dark tunnel, braked with an ear-splitting squeal, and slid to a stop alongside the platform. The doors to the car immediately in front of him opened. No one came out. The people around him rushed for the doors. Suddenly afraid that he would be left out and would miss Robin Hood's contact, he pushed forward and squeezed in with the others.

All the seats were taken by brokerage house workers who had gotten on the train at Wall Street and William. The floor space around the poles was also claimed. The car was incredibly crowded and would be until Penn Station when the stockbrokers would switch to the Penn Central or the Long Island Railroad. Therefore, Meyrowitz stood in the circular space at the confluence of both doors, shoulder-to-shoulder with a variety of New Yorkers, none of them Dunio or Powell.

He could not see any of the three agents who had boarded with him. But he imagined that they were spread out in the car, trying to watch everyone at once and, at the same time, trying to avoid one another's eyes.

Rolling sickeningly from left to right as if it were a ship wallowing in rough seas, the subway train rocketed northward under Manhattan.

A soft, lilting voice on Meyrowitz's right said, "Excuse me."

He turned and saw that he was standing next to a beautiful ash-blond girl. He had noticed her on the platform and had momentarily suspected her. But then, he suspected everyone.

"There's a shopping bag at your side," she said, speaking so softly that no one around them could have heard. "Without making a show of it, you can lower the box right into it."

He was holding the box under his arm. He let it slide down to his hip, then hooked his fingers in the binder twine, lowered it into her shopping bag, and released it.

He hoped one of the three special agents in the car had seen this quiet action. But he doubted it.

"Thank you," she said. She smiled at him. She had a stunning, obscene smile.

January 2—5:10 P.M.

When the curly-headed man dropped the box into the shopping bag, Madelaine Harlow glanced down to see if the toilet paper had been compressed as it was supposed to have been. She was gratified to see that the box had sunk down past the top of the bag.

Now what?

Now just stand and wait, she told herself.

She was losing her cool. She always tried to be as tough and self-possessed as Pia James. But she realized this box contained something like heroin, and she was thinking about spending ten years in jail if a cop grabbed her this minute.

Still, she kept cool enough to smile at the curly-headed man and say, "Don't stare down at the box. That just draws attention to it."

He met her eyes. He looked mean, angry. What the hell? He knew he was going to pass it along to someone, didn't he?

In the crush of passengers immediately behind her, someone reached out and touched Madelaine's hand, the hand that was holding the straps of the shopping bag. She almost jumped, almost turned around. But it was only Pia back there.

As the train rolled into Penn Station, Madelaine looked at the doors in front of her and let go of the shopping bag. She felt Pia ease it back a foot or two. An instant later, the straps of a second bag were slipped into her hand. This quick exchange would have been well concealed by the commuters who were standing close to Pia on all sides—especially since all the movement had been at floor level. Madelaine lifted the bag a few inches and found that this one was also puffed up with toilet paper.

The train shuddered, stopped.

The doors slid open.

When Robin Hood stepped out onto the platform in Penn Station, David Meyrowitz allowed other passengers to stream out around him. When there was some distance between him and the girl, he followed her, confident that the three agents in the car were right behind him.

Madelaine Harlow threaded her way through the home-going throng until she reached the narrow little escalator. She stepped onto it and rode to the top, came out in the main terminal concourse which was jammed with rush hour travelers.

She felt sillier than ever toting around a bag full of toilet paper, and she went hunting for a trash barrel. She found one in front of the pizza shop by the passenger benches. She stuffed the Korvettes' bag into the can, turned, and walked out toward the Seventh Avenue exit where she could get a taxi to take her home.

She heard shouting behind her, but at first she did not think that it was directed at her. If you were used to the city streets, you paid no attention to the occasional public arguments that erupted around you. But then she noticed that people coming toward her were staring first at the source of the shouting—and then at her.

Cops?

Please God, no.

Looking over her shoulder, she saw the curly-headed man who had been on the train. What was this all about? Here in the middle of Penn Station, he was actually *running* after her. If he wanted his box back, he was out of luck.

She tried to keep her cool, lost it at once. She turned and ran between the streams of incoming commuters that gushed across the huge room. Without looking back again, she made it to the wide Seventh Avenue corridor, twisted and squirmed through the crowd to the glass doors at the end. Gaining the outside escalator, she risked a glance behind her.

The curly-headed one was no longer on her trail. But three other guys were. They were big and clean-cut, and they looked like cops.

"Jesus!" she said.

It hadn't been worth three hundred dollars.

They did not follow her onto the escalator, but ran up the steps beside it. They were strong and in good shape, and they made better time than the escalator did.

When she reached the top and was propelled onto the sidewalk, they were waiting for her.

January 2—5:15 P.M.

For a brief moment Meyrowitz wondered if he should put the trashcan under surveillance and wait for Robin Hood to retrieve the shopping bag. However, he realized that the paintings might somehow have been shifted out of the bag. And if that were the case, he would just be wasting time here. He had to become a scavenger.

But the goddamned trashcan was built like a safe-deposit box. He wrestled with it and finally overturned it. He managed to tear off the domed top, spilling a rich mixture of garbage onto the terminal floor.

"Hey Mac, what the shit do you think you're doing?" A transit policeman, four inches taller and forty pounds heavier than Meyrowitz, grabbed the agent by the back of his coat and very nearly lifted him off the floor, away from the garbage.

"FBI," Meyrowitz said.

The cop blinked at him, then reddened. "Oh, sure."

"No, really," Meyrowitz said.

People were staring.

Meyrowitz wrenched himself loose from the cop who had hold of him. He went for the wallet in his inside coat pocket, pulled it out, flipped it open as the cop was grabbing for his club. "FBI, damn you!" Meyrowitz yelled. "And if you don't let me search that garbage can, I'll have your ass in a federal prison!"

The cop blinked. "Hell, search it!"

Meyrowitz realized suddenly what he had said and what the situation must look like to a passerby. He started laughing and couldn't quit. He used one foot to separate the trash and located the shopping bag. Tears streaming down his face, he lifted the bag, opened it, turned it upside-down, and dumped mounds of unraveled toilet paper onto the floor. He looked at the transit cop and at the hundred or more people who had gathered around, and he exploded into greater roars of laughter.

"Let me see that ID again," the policeman said.

Meyrowitz showed him, then said, "Excuse me." He pushed past them and hurried out through the crowd, out toward the Seventh Avenue exit where the girl had been going.

He found her with the three agents who were waiting for him in the corridor by the OTB office.

"You passed it on to someone else, didn't you?" he asked breathlessly.

"Yeah," she said. She was trembling.

"Who? And how?"

She looked around at the curious people who were rushing past and at the small group of men who had come out of the OTB place to see what was up. "Here?" she asked Meyrowitz.

"No. We'll go someplace quieter. FBI headquarters."

"Yeah," she said mournfully. "These guys already told me."

In the unmarked car parked opposite the Rialto Theater on Times Square, Roy Genelli checked his wristwatch, then studied the eight-inch screen of the electronic scanner that was mounted on the console between the halves of the front seat. The screen, gridded over with a skeleton map of mid-town Manhattan, glowed a soft green. It was quiet; no point of light flickered on it.

"Still underground," Plover said.

Agent Marks, who was leaning over watching from the back seat, said, "That means Robin Hood didn't get off that train at Penn Station."

Genelli looked at his wristwatch again, grimaced. "If we don't get a signal in two more minutes, we can figure he didn't get off at Times Square, either. Or he changed trains."

He was getting a queasy feeling in his stomach.

Remember the Zilinski-Ross case, he told himself. There were some bad moments on that one, some times when you thought you'd blown it. But you did just fine in the end.

Remember that.

The scanner remained quiet.

24.

January 2—5:35 P.M.

Carrying a Korvettes' shopping bag, Pia James left the subway train at Seventy-second and Broadway, but she did not go up to the street. Instead, she crossed to the other side of the platform and joined a group of people waiting for a downtown train.

She surveyed the crowd a couple of times but saw no one paying attention to her. It was going to be an easy five thousand bucks. Or forty-seven hundred, deducting Madelaine's payment.

For a moment she toyed with the idea of saying to hell with Dan Walters and taking the contents of the box for herself. If she got five thousand just to act as the courier for the stuff, what must it be worth? It weighed maybe a pound and a half, two pounds. Heroin? How much could she get for two pounds of pure skag? Or maybe it was cash money, all in hundreds. Diamonds?

The train came, and she got aboard.

As the doors closed and the wheels began to turn, she thought: Take your five thousand dollars and run. Are you *asking* for trouble? Who do you think Walters is, anyway? Some hick? He's probably tied in with the mob. Do you want to make *them* mad at you?

She got off the train at Twenty-third Street and Seventh Avenue, went up to the surface, and walked two blocks to her Mercedes. She was right back where she had started.

When she opened the door on the driver's side, she saw that there was a girl in the passenger's seat. "What are you doing in my car?"

"Mr. Walters asked me to meet you," the girl said.

Hesitantly, Pia James got in behind the wheel, lifted the shopping bag onto her lap, closed the door. "I thought Walters was coming himself."

"No," the girl said. "He sent me."

She was wearing too much makeup, dark glasses even though the early winter night had already fallen, and a fairly good black wig. She was very pretty, but she had no style. Any cop would have tagged her as a prostitute the moment he saw her, Pia thought. She said, "My money."

The girl passed over an envelope.

Pia looked inside it, thumbed through the bills, but did not try to count them by the light that came through the windows. "Good. Now, take the shopping bag and go."

The girl nodded. She opened her door, stepped out, reached back in and took both the Korvettes' bag and a Bloomingdale's bag which was her own. She walked across the street and turned back toward Seventh Avenue.

Relieved to be finished with her part of the deal, Pia James locked her doors, started the Mercedes, and drove away.

January 2—5:48 P.M.

Roy Genelli was ready to start ripping his gloves apart when the call finally came through from David Meyrowitz on the two-way radio.

"Car 202 calling 201," Meyrowitz said. "You read me?"

"Here!" Genelli said, snatching the microphone from the dashboard. "What in the hell went wrong?"

By this time the subway train would have reached Ninety-sixth Street and Maybe even 110th Street at Lenox Avenue. And still there had been no signal on the console monitor.

Meyrowitz said, "The woman who contacted me—"

"Woman!" Genelli said.

"Hear me out," Meyrowitz said. Static rushed in, faded. "We followed her out into Penn Station, and then we discovered she'd passed the box to someone else before she left the car."

"And none of you jackasses *noticed?*" Genelli said.

"You're feeling the ax," Meyrowitz said. "It's more complicated than I'm going to explain right now. Suffice to say it was cleverly done. Anyway, the first woman says she passed it to a second."

"Then where's that one?" Genelli asked. "She hasn't come up to street level. We're not getting any signal here."

"I don't know about that," Meyrowitz said. "But I do know who she is."

"You do?"

"Yes. We apprehended the woman here, the one I *thought* had the box. She's very talkative. Says she was hired for this by a woman named Pia James. This James is a call girl. I got her address from the woman we nabbed. I think she's a call girl too, although she says she's an actress."

"Give me the James address," Genelli said. "We'll have her place staked out."

Meyrowitz read it off to him.

"I've got it," Genelli said. "We'll—"

On the scanner beside him, a flicker of light appeared, winking like a star, and a *bleep-bleep-bleep* filled the car.

"We've got her!" he shouted into the microphone. He looked more closely at the monitor and frowned when he saw that the light was less than exact. It was fuzzy-edged and covered about half a block area on both sides of a street. "She's somewhere on Twenty-fifth, near Seventh Avenue."

His words were going out to all the cars in the operation. Cruisers would be moving up from Fourteenth Street on Eighth Avenue and down from Penn Station on Seventh.

"She's at Twenty-fourth now," Genelli said.

The light blinked on the scanner. The beacon sounded once every second.

"Twenty-third," Genelli said. "Moving toward Eighth Avenue now. Wait a minute . . . It's stationary."

"Should I move out?" Plover asked, racing the engine.

Genelli shook his head: no.

A crackling voice came over the radio: "Car 215 moving down from Penn Station."

Car 206 moving up from Fourteenth," another voice chimed in. "But the traffic's terrible. We can't make any speed unless we use the sirens."

"No sirens yet," Genelli said. "That's only a last resort."

January 2—5:56 P.M.

Little more than a minute after she had left Pia James, Carrie met Lee at the corner of Seventh Avenue and Twenty-fifth, where he was waiting in a rented Ford. Using his false papers, Powell had gotten the car on the afternoon of December thirty-first, then had parked it in a garage near the Americana Hotel where Lee had reclaimed it at five o'clock this evening. Carrie got into the passenger's seat, pulled the door shut, and put the shopping bags on the floor between her legs.

"Trouble?" Lee asked.

"No."

"Back to the Americana," he said. He accelerated into a meager break in traffic, went south and took a cross street over to the Avenue of the Americas. "You look perfect," he said, glancing at her. "Just cheap enough to seem real."

"On the way down," she said, "I got propositioned twice."

Without encountering anyone with whom she worked closely, Carrie had left her office early, at four thirty. Rather than pass the receptionist at the elevators, she had used the stairs to go down three floors. There, in a locked cubicle in the women's rest room, she had opened a Bloomingdale's bag and had dumped out the articles that she had been keeping in her office for almost a week now: the long black wig, skintight pants, cheap makeup . . . In fifteen minutes she no longer looked like herself and would not be spotted and followed by any FBI agents who might be watching the building. By five thirty she had reached Pia James's Mercedes.

Now, as Lee drove through the rush hour traffic, she opened the Korvettes' bag. Using a penknife, she cut the binder twine and slit the wrapping paper all the way around the top of the box. She pulled up the lid and lifted out five velvet-wrapped rectangles.

"Well?" Lee asked.

She pulled out the shredded paper that had been used to cushion the paintings. Down in the bottom of the box, there was a small transmitter and two penlight batteries. She showed them to Lee when they stopped for a red light.

He caught her fear and smiled to let her know she might as well relax. "In this traffic, there's no way the cops are going to pinpoint us and stop the car this soon. If at all." He felt better than he had in the last three years. "Everything's flowing like hot molasses."

She put the empty box with its miniaturized transmitter back into the shopping bag, slipped the paintings into the attaché case that lay on the seat beside Lee. She closed the case, thumbed down the latches.

As the car weaved in and out of traffic on its way up the Avenue of the Americas, she watched the people on the sidewalks and tried to calm herself and wondered when her heart would finally explode from the strain.

January 2—6:05 P.M.

"They're obviously in a car," Genelli said into the microphone. "Maybe a taxi. Moving up Sixth Avenue . . ."

On the monitor screen, a fleck of light pulsed across the map of the city like a firefly buzzing smoothly along a lighted window.

"Fortieth Street," Genelli said.

Bleep . . . bleep . . . bleep . . .

"Car 215 from Penn Station," a voice cut in on the line. "I moved over to Sixth, and I'm at Thirty-eighth . . . What the hell should I look for if I can close the gap? You sure it's a cab we're after?"

"No," Genelli said. "I don't know. Just keep your eyes open."

Bleep . . . bleep . . .

"Car 206," another voice said.

"Go ahead 206."

"I'm at Eighth Avenue at Fiftieth. Traffic hasn't been so bad over here. Since I'm ahead of the target, you want me to try to cut across to Sixth and intercept him?"

"Negative," Genelli said. "They may turn and come your way. And you wouldn't know who to intercept anyway. Stay on Eighth, but slow down."

He looked at the console, watched the spot of light move past Forty-second Street, then past Forty-third, crawling relentlessly up the Avenue of the Americas toward Forty-fourth.

"Doesn't look like he's going to turn this way," Genelli said.

"Sure doesn't," Plover agreed.

"Even if he does," Marks said, "there are five other cruisers in the Times Square area."

Genelli looked over at Plover. "See if you can get across to Sixth and fall in behind them."

"Hold on," Plover said.

Although the light was about to change, Plover tramped on the accelerator. The rear tires screamed, and the sedan shot away from the curb.

The light changed, and a taxi started to cross their path on Seventh Avenue. The driver saw them coming, slammed on his brakes, and pulled his cab into the median barrier where it struck with a jolt. Horns blared on all sides.

Plover wheeled across Broadway, narrowly missing a gray Volvo and terrifying a pretzel vender who was trying to cross the street with his cart. At the southwest corner of Broadway and Forty-second, he almost clipped two Hare Krishna youths in their soiled robes, sweat socks, and tennis shoes.

"Jesus!" Marks said, from the back seat.

Plover was grinning.

Halfway down the block between Broadway and Sixth, a sidewalk patrolman who had seen them careen through the intersection stepped out into the street to try to stop them. He blew on his whistle and waved both arms at them.

"Don't kill him!" Genelli shouted.

Plover swung the sedan hard to the left, out past the middle line of Forty-second Street. They roared past the cop and scattered all the traffic ahead of them.

Plover made the light at Sixth Avenue, though just barely, and then he began to dodge through the traffic as if he had spent the last thirty years behind the wheel of a New York City cab.

25.

January 2—6:15 P.M.

Lee pulled the Ford to the curb at the Fifty-third Street entrance to the Americana Hotel. "Park it up on Twenty-fourth and walk down from there," he reminded her.

As he got out, she slid over behind the wheel. She handed him the attaché case and the Korvettes' bag. "Careful."

"You too," he said, closing the door.

As she worked her way back into the traffic flow, he walked over to a nearby public trash can where he threw away the shopping bag and the box that contained the miniaturized transmitter.

The wind had picked up in the last hour and a half, whistling through the canyons formed by the skyscrapers; the night was bitter. His long-haired wig flapped about his cheeks, and the cold stung his whole face. When he pushed through the revolving doors into the hotel lobby, however, he was flushed and not the least bit chilled.

He strode quickly across the lobby to the main stairs, went down to the basement level. He passed the Columbian Coffee Shop, turned the corner of the corridor into a longer hall, walked the length of that to the public rest rooms.

In the privacy of a men's room stall, with the door closed and latched, he opened the attaché case on his knees. Carefully unwrapping the paintings one at a time, he checked them for self-contained transmitters like that Carrie had found in the box.

The velvet cloth around the fourth painting was equipped with an incredibly tiny transmitter. It was much smaller than the one in the box had been; it was powered by a tiny Hamilton atomic battery of the sort found in better watches. The whole works was about the diameter of his littlest fingernail and as thick as two pennies.

Very clever.

He put the five paintings back in the attaché case. He stood up and raised the lid on the commode. Smiling, he dropped the micro-miniaturized transmitter into the bowl, watched it sink to the bottom, then flushed it down the john.

Let them follow it now.

Plover had them to Fifty-first Street, within two blocks of the beacon—and, therefore, within two blocks of Robin Hood—when the bleeping split into two distinct notes, and the light on the scanner screen broke apart.

"They've left the box somewhere," Genelli said, "and they're carrying the paintings in something else. The two transmitters are far enough apart that the big one isn't masking the smaller one anymore."

BLEEP . . . bleep . . . BLEEP . . . bleep . . .

"Where'd they leave the box?" Marks asked.

Genelli studied the lighted grid. "It looks like . . . On Fifty-third, halfway between Sixth and Seventh."

"And the paintings?" Like Plover, Marks knew a ransom was being paid, although he did not know how much and for what.

Genelli peered closely at the screen. "The transmitter on the paintings is just a little farther down the block, moving toward Seventh Avenue."

Plover tried to squeeze between a delivery van and a Cadillac, was cut off by one of the ubiquitous taxis. He pounded his horn.

The cabbie looked in his rear-view mirror, then gave Plover the finger.

"The bastard!" Plover said.

Two minutes later, when they reached Fifty-third Street, one of the transmitters had stopped sending. The dimmer light had disappeared from the console, and the weaker of the two electronic signals ceased to echo in the car.

"Lost him!" Genelli said.

Plover swung the car to the curb and parked on the right-hand side of the street, halfway down the block. He joined the other two in their tense vigil over the glowing scanner screen.

"How could we lose him?" Marks asked.

"Maybe he found and destroyed the beacon," Genelli said. "Or went underground again."

Only one fleck of light pulsed on the grid, and it was motionless.

"If he went into a building," Marks said, "would we still pick up the broadcast?"

"Sure," Genelli said. "As long as there's a window in the room."

"We have two hotels here," Marks observed. "The Americana in front of us, the Hilton behind us."

"Hotels have windows," Genelli said. He was beginning to feel depressed again.

"Hotels might have windows," Marks said. "But elevators don't."

Genelli perked up. "My God, you may be right." He wiped one hand over his face, stared at the screen again. "If the transmitter's in an elevator, it'll only be blocked out for a few minutes."

A minute passed more slowly than Genelli would have believed possible.

Bleep . . . *bleep* . . . *bleep* . . . Just the transmitter in the box . . .

Another minute, slower than the first had been.

The screen glowed softly; all on it was still.

"Come on," Genelli said.

Another minute. Another . . .

"*Shit!*" Genelli said.

Robin Hood had vanished.

26.

January 2—6:35 P.M.

Carrie parked the rented car on Twenty-fourth Street between Seventh and Eighth Avenues, switched off the headlights.

All things considered, she had a surprising degree of privacy there in the car. The sidewalks were nearly deserted. Because of the bitter cold, nobody was out walking by choice, and those who did pass by were walking with their heads down, faces averted from the whip of the wind. The drivers of the cars that whisked past were intent on the traffic and did not glance her way.

In the darkened Ford, Carrie became herself again. She removed the black wig and combed out her own hair. She took a jar of cold cream and a wad of tissues from her purse, wiped away all the makeup. From the Bloomingdale's bag, she took the slacks that she had worn to work and pulled them on over the skintight pants that were such a part of her prostitute persona. She struggled out of the flashy imitation fur jacket of the call girl, put on her own worn, lined raincoat. The wig and the vulgar clothes just fit in the shopping bag.

Taking the bag with her, she got out of the car, locked it, and walked down to the apartment on Twentieth Street.

January 2—6:48 P.M.

Agent Wickstrom, one of the two men watching the front entrance to the Ackridge-Hoffman apartment house, drummed his fingers on his knee and wondered what was taking the communications man so long up there on East Sixty-ninth Street.

Then the call came through.

"Go ahead," Wickstrom said.

"I've talked to each team of agents who're watching that office building," the headquarters man said, his voice distorted by static on the line. "They all report negative. She hasn't yet left work."

"Like hell," Wickstrom said. "We just saw her come home. Now why weren't we warned that she'd left work? Who missed her up there?"

"Nobody will admit it," the headquarters man said.

"Now," Wickstrom said, "the question is did she make an effort to slip by them, or did they just miss her in the rush?"

"You want me to get this to Genelli?"

Wickstrom thought a moment. Then: "Yeah. Ask him if we should just continue surveillance or whether we should go upstairs and have a talk with Miss Hoffman."

"Will do," the headquarters man said. "I'll be back to you in a few minutes."

"Make it fast," Wickstrom said. He put down the microphone.

"Probably nothing to it," Agent Wagner said, slouching down behind the wheel of the Bureau car.

"Probably," Wickstrom agreed. "But we can't take chances."

January 2—7:00 P.M.

Slightly numbed by the near-zero temperatures, Douglas Powell returned from his hour-long walk in the woods and went into the house by way of the kitchen door where he had forced entry early in the afternoon. Even inside the house, his breath frosted in front of him, and his nose watered.

The cold was the only thing he had not expected, and he was surprised he had overlooked it. He had *known* there would not be any lights, that the electricity would be switched off; and he had been prepared for that. The house and the fourteen wooded acres which went with it belonged to close friends of the general and sweet Loretta. The Jamisons, old Ernie and Marge. The Jamisons always spent December, January, and February in Florida, and during those months their house was closed up tight, deserted. But he had forgotten that an oil furnace was electrically ignited, and now he had to suffer for his shortsightedness.

He opened the box of two dozen fifteen-hour votive candles, and he began to light them with long wooden matches. He set a dozen candles on the dark pine kitchen table and spotted the others all over the room: one beside the water faucet at the sink, one on the drainboard, one on top of the refrigerator, two more on the stove . . . The twenty-four tongues of fire cast dancing, hobgoblin shadows on the walls and against the black windows.

He sat down at the table and looked at his wristwatch. He had a long wait ahead of him.

But by this time, he suddenly thought, it was all finished in New York. And they were one step closer to wrapping it up. He smiled, laughed aloud, and sat for several minutes savoring his triumph in advance.

Candlelight flickered on his long face and made glowing coals of his eyes.

He felt as if he had popped some pills, as if he were high on speed and bursting with nervous energy. He wanted to shout and scream. Most of all, he wanted to burn himself out in hard, physical activity: running, jumping, breaking things . . .

Knocking over his chair, he stood up.

He had to get out of this cold, nearly lightless room. He could feel the terrible weight of the rest of the big house pressing down on him.

He went outside and looked down the driveway on his left, then to the woods straight ahead. The serenity of the night calmed him. After a while he started going over in his mind just where he would pretend, to Dunio, that his armed guards were stationed. He intended to tell Dunio there were four of them.

It wasn't that he distrusted the ex-sergeant. But there *was* a fortune involved . . .

January 2—7:20 P.M.

Lee Ackridge entered his apartment house just as he had left it: through the adjoining buildings. Behind a dusty old cabinet in the basement of his own house, he hid the attaché case that contained the paintings. Then he went up to the third floor where Carrie was waiting for him.

She hugged him tightly.

"Everything's fine," he said.

"Did they have the paintings bugged?"

"Yeah. But I took care of that."

"They're outside in an unmarked car," she said. "I looked for them without being obvious about it."

"I better get out of this costume," he said. "They'll probably be knocking on the door before much longer."

She followed him back down the hall and stood in the doorway of the bathroom while he unwound his scarf, stripped out of his coat, pulled off the long-haired wig, and washed the makeup from his scarred face.

"Better put the wig with the black one, on your side of the closet," he said.

She did that. When she came back, she said, "Where'd you stash the paintings?"

"Basement," he said. "What about the shopping bag you carried in with you?"

"As planned," she said. "I took care of the contents. Then I put half a dozen books in it, the ones I bought Saturday. If they want to know what I bought, I'll let them look over the books as long as they want." She grinned. "None of it's subversive literature."

"And when they want to know how you left work without their men seeing you?"

"How should I know that?" she asked. "I mean, I left with everyone else. It's a real exodus around five o'clock. Maybe they just missed me in the rush."

"You sound pretty good. If they ask—"

The doorbell rang.

"It's them," he said.

She said, "I'll get it. Just relax now."

"Sure."

January 2—7:45 P.M.

Pia James's Fifth Avenue apartment, which overlooked Central Park, was paved with expensive carpet, filled with expensive furniture, and decorated with original oil paintings. All the colors flowed together, and the angles of the furniture complemented the angles of the rooms. The final effect was one of warm sensuality, an extension of the woman herself.

Having watched her in the living room for more than half an hour as six of his men searched the rest of her apartment, Genelli was still unable to reconcile her appearance and personality with her profession. With a starlet's shape, dazzling green eyes, and naturally black hair, she was most certainly beautiful enough to be able to put a high price on her body. But there was nothing *hard* about her, none of the tough look of a prostitute; indeed, she was almost wholesome. Furthermore, she was clearly well-read, cultured, intelligent, sensitive . . . She was no whore with a heart of gold, but neither was she what he expected.

She had revealed the nature and length of her career in answer to his first question. He had not begun to interrogate her until his men had finished searching her apartment with the full authority of the warrant Genelli had shown her. He had hoped that if she sat there and stewed for half an hour, she would begin to come apart. But she was cool, straightforward, and utterly unshaken.

"Is your name really Pia James?" Genelli asked.

"The James part is real. My first name's actually Peggy."

Meyrowitz took notes.

"I must warn you, Miss James, that whatever you say may be used against you, and that you have the right—"

"Ask whatever you want," she said. "I won't hide anything, because I haven't done anything illegal."

He questioned her about her activities between five and six o'clock, and she responded with candor.

"And you don't think you've done anything illegal?" David Meyrowitz asked, looking up from his notebook.

"I didn't know what was in the box."

"Doesn't matter," Meyrowitz said.

"I still don't know," she said.

"It's doubtful that your ignorance would convince a jury to look upon you as blameless," Genelli said.

"Not blameless," she agreed, sipping her drink. "But at most, I'd get sent up for a couple of months, serve some nuisance time."

Meyrowitz shook his head in admiration.

"You've mentioned a Mr. Walters," Genelli said.

"Yes."

"Are you certain the man who hired you was not named Powell?"

"Walters was just a name he used with me. I don't know what his real name is."

Taking a photograph of Dunio from the nine-by-twelve envelope that he had brought with him, Genelli passed it to her.

"Never saw him before," she said.

"You're sure?"

"Yes."

He took the photograph back and handed her another one, leaned forward on his chair in anticipation of her answer.

"That's Dan Walters," she said.

It was Douglas Powell.

Genelli felt a rush of adrenalin pouring into his system, and he fought down an overwhelming urge to get up and *move.* He had a few more questions to put to her. "You say the girl to whom you gave the box, the girl who was waiting for you in your car on Twenty-fifth, was another prostitute?"

"An obvious one," Pia James said with distaste.

"Give us a description."

She did.

Meyrowitz wrote it down.

"You'd never seen her before?" Genelli asked.

"No."

"Do you think Madelaine Harlow would know her?"

"I doubt it," Pia James said. "This girl looked very young, maybe eighteen. She probably got into the city within the last month or two. Somebody new."

He asked several more questions, and she answered them as fully as she had all the others.

Thrusting his notebook in his coat pocket, David Meyrowitz said, "*I* have a question."

"Yes?" she asked, picking the cherry out of her drink with thumb and forefinger and delicately popping it into her mouth.

He stood up beside Genelli and stared down at her. "A small army of FBI agents descends on you all unexpected, searches your apartment from one end to the other, and questions you for more than forty-five minutes . . . And not once have you asked what this Dan Walters has done. Why not?"

She finished chewing the cherry, frowned at him, clasped her drink in both hands and held it against her heavy breasts. "I simply don't want to know," she said rather haughtily. "It would just be something sordid and depressing."

January 2—8:15 P.M.

Agent Wickstrom watched the apartment building on Twentieth Street while he spoke to the communications man up on Sixty-ninth. "She was a little late getting home, because she stopped to buy a few books."

"That's what was in the shopping bag?" the headquarters man asked, his voice fading slightly on the line.

"Yeah," Wickstrom said. "So it looks like the boys watching her office goofed."

"You believe her?"

"No reason to disbelieve. They were both real surprised to hear we were tailing them. They can't understand what Powell could have done to make his friends so suspect. I don't think they were acting, either."

"Ackridge hasn't gone out all day?" the headquarters man asked.

"Right. There's been movement up there, lights going on and off, since late afternoon."

"Well," the operator said, "*he's* the suspect. If you believe her, and if he's been home all day, I guess we can rule them out."

"Good enough," Wickstrom said.

"But maintain surveillance."

"Naturally." Wickstrom hung up the microphone.

Wagner, who was sitting behind the wheel, said, "They seemed like a real nice couple."

"Yeah," Wickstrom said. "Didn't she have beautiful eyes?"

JANUARY 2, 9:00 P.M.– MIDNIGHT

Princeton

27.

January 2—9:00 P.M.

They were both disguised again. Lee was wearing his bulky coat, scarf, and long-haired wig, although he had not used any of the stage makeup to tone down his scars. Carrie was wearing the long black wig, tight pants, short fur coat. She, too, had not bothered with the makeup. If any of those men outside came close enough to see Lee's scars or to recognize her face, they were finished anyway.

"Ready?" he asked.

She nodded.

They left the apartment, went down to the basement, where he retrieved the attaché case from behind the cabinet. Using a flashlight to cut a path through the intense darkness, they went from one cellar to the next until they reached the third building. Moving quietly, cautiously, they went up to the first floor of that apartment house, through the foyer, and outside.

The wind was harsh and cold.

At the bottom of the steps, they turned in the opposite direction from the Bureau car and their own building, walked out to the avenue, and turned uptown.

No one stopped them.

At Twenty-fourth Street they returned to the rented Ford. The car had succumbed to the sweeping wind and low temperatures, and it did not want to start. At last, just when the battery seemed about to conk out, the engine caught and chugged raggedly.

Lee maneuvered the car out of its tightly bracketed parking slot and headed east, studying the rearview mirror as he drove.

"Anyone back there?" Carrie asked.

"I don't think so."

At Sixth Avenue he turned left and went uptown, still keeping an eye on the street behind him. Nobody followed him out of Twenty-fourth. But here on the avenue, there was some traffic, and it was difficult for him to tell if any of the cars behind him was running a tail.

At Thirty-ninth Street he turned west into a heavier flow of cars and struck out for the Lincoln Tunnel. He had the crazy notion, as they grew closer to the tunnel, that there would be a police roadblock waiting for them.

There was none, of course.

Twenty minutes later, when they were well onto the New Jersey Turnpike, he sighed with relief.

"Well?" she asked hopefully.

"We aren't being followed," he said, grinning broadly.

She relaxed. "We ought to reach the estate by eleven thirty. It's almost finished."

He nodded and was surprised to feel a pang of regret.

January 2—10:30 P.M.

"The main reason I've stuck with this crummy diplomatic duty all these years," Agent Ashe explained to Agent Packer, "is because you never pull an extended shift here like you do on the other kinds of assignments. Hell, even when that Air Force captain ran off with his folder full of airplane plans, we didn't pull extended shifts on diplomatic duty. So what the fuck are they doing to me tonight?"

Ashe and Packer had been put on a twelve-hour work assignment. They were to tail Ilya Zaitsev from ten o'clock at night until ten in the morning, in order to free other agents for Genelli's task force.

Naturally, no one had explained to Ashe and Packer just what this emergency alert was all about. And though Packer was taking it as a matter of course, Ashe couldn't see the necessity behind it, and he was disgruntled.

However, when the radio carried the news of the warrant for Douglas Powell's arrest, Ashe stopped complaining. "That's interesting," he said. "The Russian is up early every morning, eats breakfast at the Plaza around seven or seven thirty. But you know that . . . Anyway, my old partner and I saw this Powell kid join him for breakfast a couple of times."

"Oh?"

"Headquarters looked into it. Said Powell had met Zaitsev at several Washington parties two years ago. They're just casual friends. But now, I wonder—"

Packer interrupted him. "Zaitsev just came out."

Ashe looked across the street at the Russian.

The liveried doorman whistled down a cab, held the door for Zaitsev, shut it after him, and went quickly back inside where it was warm. The taxi sped north on Central Park West, turned left onto Sixty-eighth Street.

"I *knew* there'd be excitement tonight," Packer said, giving chase.

When they turned the corner, the taxi was only half a block ahead.

"Slow down," Ashe said. "Don't want to be too obvious."

They trailed the cab to Amsterdam Avenue, then south to Tenth Avenue. As they were passing Fiftieth Street, Packer said, "Maybe I'm crazy, but I don't think anyone's in that cab but the driver."

As Packer spoke, the taxi pulled over to pick up a fare.

"Damn!" Ashe said. "Block him off!"

Packer wheeled in front of the cab, bouncing tires on the curb.

Ashe was out of the cruiser the instant it stopped, and Packer was right behind him.

"What the hell?" the cabbie wanted to know.

"FBI," Ashe said, flashing credentials. "Where's the Russian?"

The cabbie was perplexed. "Russian?"

"The fare you picked up five minutes ago on Central Park West," Ashe said impatiently.

"Jesus!" the driver said, turning pale. "I didn't know he was Russian. I'd never have—"

"*Where is he?*" Ashe demanded.

"Paid me ten bucks to drive him around the corner from his apartment house," the driver said. "I thought he was trying to lose a jealous husband or somethin'. He said he—"

Ashe turned away, ran for the Bureau car, calling for Packer to move ass.

Sliding in behind the wheel, Packer said, "What now?"

"I think I know where Zaitsev's going."

"You do?"

"He keeps a car in a garage in one of those alleyways off Fiftieth

Street." He gave Packer directions, held on as the other agent accelerated toward Eighth Avenue. "He keeps the car registered under a false name in New Jersey."

"And we let him?" Packer asked, wheeling through a changing light, streaking toward Eighth.

"Sure. He has to have a car he thinks is a big secret. Better that we let him have one we know about than one we don't."

Packer turned the car onto Eighth, running a red light. On Fiftieth they came up behind Zaitsev's car almost before Ashe knew it.

"That's him!"

Packer fell back more than a block behind the three-year-old Dodge the Russian was driving.

"I better call in," Ashe said. "We may need help."

28.

January 2—10:50 P.M.

"It's not just your career that's at stake—or mine. *Christ*, Genelli, if that stolen data isn't recovered, everybody in this country goes down the drain together!" Gardner Peterson slammed one fist against the top of the desk to emphasize what he had said.

The supervisor had lost most of his characteristic dignity. Red-faced, his hair no longer neatly combed, he was clearly on the edge of desperation. His tie was askew. He had forsaken his jacket hours ago, and his trousers were badly wrinkled. He was perspiring, though not because the room was hot. He was suffering from a heat that emanated from Washington and which was directed specifically against the back of his neck.

Genelli recalled Meyrowitz's warning, and he realized it was now time for scapegoats to be identified. "I've got every remote acquaintance of Powell under surveillance. I've got men going through the hotel records in the area where Robin Hood disappeared with the paintings. I—"

Peterson interrupted him. "If those tapes are passed on to *anyone,* friend or enemy alike, they'll be used against us. There isn't a country in the world that would hesitate to step on the United States to enhance its own position. At the very least, we'll be blackmailed. If you've botched this one, Genelli, it'll go down in the history books as—"

"I've heard enough," Genelli said sharply. Adversity did not affect him in the same way as it did Peterson. In a crisis he did not lose dignity but gained it. He no longer gave the impression of being as plain and uninteresting as the brown suit he wore. He was tougher and sharper than he had been in years, honed by the events of the last two days. "I *know* how bad the situation is," he told Peterson. "It's a waste of time for you to lecture me and for me to listen."

Peterson scowled. "Now just a minute—"

"Maybe, if there hadn't been a delay in getting that warrant for Powell, we'd have gotten a lead by now. Maybe not. All we can do is hang tight and wait for something—"

A messenger from the data correlation room rushed into Genelli's office, but stopped short when he realized that Peterson and Genelli were shouting at each other. He looked at Meyrowitz who was standing by the window and watching the altercation as if it were being staged strictly for his entertainment.

Meyrowitz exchanged a glance with the messenger, shrugged.

Catching sight of the agent out of the corner of his eye, Genelli turned and said, "What is it?"

The messenger looked from Genelli to the supervisor, then back at Genelli again. "At 10:43, Communications got a radio report from a diplomatic tail following a Russian who works at the United Nations. Communications passed the report to us, and it checked out. I think we've really got something."

"*What?*" Genelli asked impatiently.

"Five times in the last six months," the messenger said, "Douglas Powell has met this Russian—name's Ilya Zaitsev—for breakfast at the Plaza. And now the routine tail assigned to Zaitsev says the Russian has proceeded to a garage where he keeps a car registered to him under a phony name, and he's leaving Manhattan."

Genelli looked at Meyrowitz.

The young agent said, "This is it."

"You think he's going somewhere to meet Powell?" Peterson demanded.

"It's the only lead we have," Genelli said.

Peterson frowned. "But Zaitsev must know he's watched. Why would he risk being seen in public with Powell if they were cooking up this theft?"

"Maybe Zaitsev didn't realize there was an agent *in* the Plaza every morning, watching to see who had breakfast with him," the messenger said.

Genelli took Ilya Zaitsev's background report from the messenger's hands and gave it to the supervisor. "You better put someone on it."

Peterson said, "You, of course."

Genelli shook his head. "Half an hour ago, when you first walked in here, you said you were taking me off the case. Don't you remember?"

Peterson was not as angry as he was horrified by Genelli's tone. "I *want* you on this."

Genelli knew that was true, and he smiled sourly. Peterson wanted him on it right up to the bitter end. If this Zaitsev thing led nowhere, if they botched the Robin Hood case, the supervisor would need someone onto whom he could shift the full blame. And who was better for that than easy-going Roy?

At that moment, Genelli knew he was finished in the Bureau whether or not he cracked this case. From now on, there would be no fun in the work, no sense of accomplishment at all.

Nevertheless, he said, "I'll stay with it as long as I can have whatever I need. If any more warrants are called for, I want them issued fast."

"Naturally."

Genelli turned to Meyrowitz and saw the pitying smile on the younger man's face. "I can't help it," he said. "I'm an old plow horse who just *has* to plod along to the end of the row before he can collapse."

Meyrowitz laughed. "Me too, I suppose."

"Get Plover," Genelli said. "We're going to catch up with the car that's on Zaitsev's tail. We'll make a regular parade out of it."

January 2—11:10 P.M.

At the estate west of Princeton, a fine dry snow had begun to fall. A thin and ghostly skirt of it swirled on the ground; but the sky was low and solidly overcast, and the skirt would soon become a coat several inches thick.

Douglas Powell was standing at the kitchen window watching the snow hiss across the outside of the glass and pile up in the corners of the window frame, when Dunio arrived. The black Cadillac came hesitantly up the long driveway, headlights slicing open the night like twin scalpels parting flesh. It parked fifty feet from the side of the house.

In addition to Dunio, three men got out of the car, and they immediately fanned out, putting space between themselves. Two of them were armed with pistols, and the third carried a Thompson submachine gun which had an eerie, insectile appearance in the darkness and the snow. The man with the submachine gun stood by the car where he could command a view of the house and the woods. One of the others went to Powell's right and stood at the corner of the house where he could watch two sides of it. The third guard came with Dunio to the kitchen door.

Powell opened for them.

"Hello, Doug," Dunio said. He was five-nine, extremely broad-shouldered, with a thick chest and the look of a gorilla stuffed into a suit.

"Come in," Powell said.

"Why're the lights out?" Dunio asked.

"People who own the place are in Florida for the winter. The power's cut off while they're gone."

"You alone in there?"

"Yes. But I've got men in the woods."

Dunio nodded. "That's O.K. I expect that."

He and his guard came into the candlelit kitchen, bringing with them an eddy of snowflakes.

The guard was handsome, slim, and tall. If this were a movie, Powell thought, the handsome guard would have had the part of the smuggler, while the burly and somewhat slavic-looking Dunio would be the cheap muscle.

When Powell closed the door and turned around, he found them standing in the center of the room, facing him. The guard was aiming an automatic at Powell's chest.

"One thing upsets me," Dunio said. "I don't know what you've done to get these paintings, but I want to know how in the hell my name got mixed up in it."

Powell was genuinely puzzled.

"We heard it on the car radio, on the hourly news," Dunio said. "There's warrants out for your arrest and mine."

"On what charges?"

"That's what I don't understand," Dunio said. "We're supposed to have killed two FBI agents in New York."

Powell almost smiled. The FBI had decided that Dunio was his partner in the data heist. Lee Ackridge would be in the clear, unless he got careless with all of his newfound wealth and drew attention to himself. "I can assure you no agents were killed. They put that on the warrant, because they were afraid to put the true charge against me. I've broken national security laws." He saw Dunio wince. "You won't have to know about that; in fact, you're better off *not* knowing. You're wanted, because they've studied my past and found I knew a man who dealt in stolen art in Asia. Naturally, they've tied this in with you." He shrugged. "What's it matter to you? You aren't Harold Dunio anymore. And you'll never be Dunio again. That man's dead. That name'll lead them nowhere."

"Just the same," Dunio said, "it bugged me to hear about that warrant. I felt like maybe you'd used me."

"How?"

"I didn't know," Dunio said, frowning. "That's what bugged me the most."

"Just cool down," Powell said.

"I guess so," Dunio said. "I've never been wanted in this country before, but I suppose the profit makes it worthwhile."

The guard lowered his pistol, pointed it at the floor.

They drew up chairs at the candle-dotted table and sat like a trio of spell-working necromancers in the shadows.

"Did you bring my papers?" Doug asked.

"Sure," Dunio said. He opened the briefcase that he was carrying and removed from it a thick white folder. He passed the folder to Powell. "Birth certificate, passport, national health insurance card, driver's license, marriage license and subsequent divorce decree, half a dozen other things. Your name is Philip Cawley, and you are a Canadian citizen. Same age as you really are. Born in a suburb of Montreal . . . It's all there."

In the weak light, Doug Powell looked over the contents of the folder. Everything seemed to be in order.

"But what was wrong with your Daniel Walters identification?" Dunio asked.

"My own name's going to be ruined in this caper," Powell said. "And the Walters identity can be too easily traced to me."

"Then the Cawley moniker isn't just a convenience. It's a necessity."

"That's right," Powell said.

From now on, he would live under the name of Cawley—if he were not apprehended when he tried to leave the country. He would attempt to start a whole new life with his share of the pay-off; he would move out and would watch the national agony —as well as the general's and Loretta's agony—from afar, where he could enjoy it fully. At least, that was what he planned to do. However, if he were nailed by the police before he could put the plan into operation, it wouldn't matter so much. He was ready for all of that: prison, a public trial . . . Increasingly over the last few days, he had come to care less and less whether or not he escaped. The important thing was ruining the general. That accomplishment was worth any price.

"Where are the paintings?" Dunio asked.

"They're on their way," Powell said. He stared at Dunio's briefcase and decided it was too small to contain a half million in cash. "Where's the money?"

"Out in the car," Dunio said.

Powell smiled and leaned back in his chair, holding the white folder on his lap. "The paintings will be here within half an hour. We'll just have to wait for them. Anyway, it gives us a chance to talk about the old days."

"Sure," Dunio said.

Neither of them spoke again in the next twenty minutes.

29.

January 2—11:40 P.M.

The wind howled around the house like an animal searching for a way to get inside, and the hard-driven snow tapped and scratched at the window panes. Several cool drafts found their way into the kitchen and stirred the two dozen candle flames until the shadows of the five people in the room leaped and danced as wildly as a ring of savages cavorting around a sacrificial fire.

"Very nice," Dunio murmured, studying the first of the five paintings which were laid out on the table.

The flashlight beam moved to the second watercolor and held on a scene of terraced hillsides and twisted trees which were all shrouded in snow that, owing to the artist's incredible talent, seemed more real than that which was actually falling just beyond the windows.

"Genuine?" Powell asked nervously.

"Wait," Dunio said.

Lee had been watching Doug closely since he and Carrie had arrived less than ten minutes ago, and he did not like what he saw. Doug was much too nervous, strung out, as if he might fly to pieces at any moment.

"If those sonsofbitches tried to pass off a bunch of fakes on us," Powell said, "I'll—"

"They wouldn't risk forgeries," Lee said. "Not with what we've got hanging over their heads. And even if they had considered it, they wouldn't have had time to forge a set of paintings that would fool an art authority."

Dunio vigorously wiped the fingers of his right hand on a clean handkerchief until he was certain that no natural oils or perspiration remained on the skin. Then he reached out reverently and touched the surface of the paintings, assured himself of the age and fragility of the silk. "So exquisite," he said.

"The real thing?" Powell insisted.

Dunio examined the third painting with an unruffled deliberation which Lee admired. Finally: "They are all genuine Ku K'ai-Chih watercolor originals."

"You're sure?" Doug asked.

Dunio nodded. "My specialty is oriental art, primarily Chinese and Chinese derivatives. Furthermore, the buyer I've lined up told me several nearly fool-proof ways to recognize a Ku K'ai-Chih."

"Who is your buyer?" Carrie asked.

Smiling, Dunio said, "Just as it is wise for me not to know how you got hold of these, it's wise for you not to know where they'll be going."

"What about the other two?" Powell asked, directing Dunio's attention back to the paintings.

Unconsciously squinting through the imprecise, wavering illumination from the flashlight, Dunio examined the last two pieces of art.

Lee watched the circle of light move over the watercolors, and he listened to the wind. He cast one quick glance at Doug and saw that Powell was perspiring in spite of the biting cold.

"Yes," Dunio said at last, drawing everyone's attention back to him. "Northern Sung Dynasty. No doubt about it. The artist was Ho Kung-yi."

Lee looked at Carrie.

She grinned back at him.

He felt as if he owned the world. He was no longer powerless, but extremely powerful.

Sighing with relief, wiping one gloved hand across his forehead, Doug Powell said, "Then we have a deal."

"We do indeed," Dunio said, nodding vigorously. "In fact, it's going to be the largest deal I've ever made." He turned to his bodyguard. "Get the suitcase from the car."

The tall, handsome man went out to the Cadillac and returned with a brown Samsonite overnight case. He put it down on the kitchen table from which Dunio had carefully gathered up the five paintings in his brief absence.

Using a brass key to unlock the case, Dunio popped the latches, lifted the lid, and revealed stacks and stacks of neatly bound United States currency.

Lee saw mostly packages of hundreds. A few stacks of fifties. Even fewer twenties.

Half a million dollars! he thought triumphantly. And it was only a fraction of what the full pay-off would be. They would see nine times as much money as this when Dunio made the main payment two weeks from now. Four and a half million *more* to come!

"Lovely," Carrie said.

"Isn't it?" Dunio asked. "Almost as lovely as the paintings." He smiled first at Doug and then at Lee. "Shall we count it and be certain it's as genuine as the paintings are?"

They did not do a complete count, but riffled each packet to make sure that the denomination of the bills in the center of each bundle was the same as those on the outer ends. As they counted, they separated the money into two piles, one for Lee and one for Doug Powell.

Five minutes after they had started, Dunio said, "Satisfied?"

"Looks good," Powell said.

"It should hold you for two weeks if you're careful not to spend it on things you don't need," Dunio said archly. "And speaking of two weeks, what do you say we meet in Toronto on the sixteenth to conclude the deal?"

"Toronto?" Carrie asked.

"I've got new papers," Powell explained. "They establish me as a Canadian citizen. I ought to be able to safely pass two weeks in Toronto before I make for Europe."

"Toronto it is, then," Lee said.

Dunio suggested the name of a good hotel in downtown Toronto where they could complete the second stage of the pay-off. When they agreed with him on that, he said, "It's sure to be more comfortable than this has been. At least we'll have heat and lights in a hotel!" He looked at Powell and shivered. "Doug, why in the hell did you insist on meeting here?"

Stiffening noticeably, Powell glanced at Lee, then looked guiltily away. "Well . . . I thought it would be private."

"A graveyard's private too," Dunio said. "But I don't care to do business in one."

Frowning, Lee said to Dunio, "I thought *you* were the one who chose this place."

"Me?" Dunio asked. "Hell, no! I wanted—"

"Lee, I'll explain myself later," Doug said. He put one arm around Dunio's shoulder and steered him toward the door.

The bodyguard followed them out into the snow and over to the gleaming Cadillac.

Standing in the eerily lighted kitchen and looking out through the open door, Lee said, "I wonder what this is all about?"

"He lied to us," Carrie said. She put one arm around Lee's waist. "He scares me."

"Scares you?"

"Did you watch his face when Dunio was inspecting the paintings? It's like before—the night we went to Langhorn. His expression changes rapidly and without reason, as if his thoughts are a chaotic mess."

"He's certainly been acting funny," Lee said. "But there's nothing to be scared of."

The Cadillac started up, made a circle in the snow, and went down the driveway, disappeared over the brow of the hill.

When Doug Powell came back, he had one of the Colt revolvers in his hand. He pointed it between Lee and Carrie, so that he could swing it quickly toward either of them. "Sit down," he said. "I'll explain the situation.

Ilya Zaitsev drove west on Route 571 toward Princeton. Agents Ashe and Packer followed at better than a quarter of a mile, sometimes falling back even farther. Genelli, Meyrowitz, and Plover trailed fifty yards behind the first Bureau car. The road was covered with an inch or more of snow, and the three cars continually slid off on the shoulder of the highway and weaved into the other lane.

After one particularly sickening slide, Meyrowitz said, "Plover, where did you learn to drive? Miami?"

"You want the wheel?" Plover asked.

"If he's done with as little sleep as I have in the past two days," Genelli said, "then his driving is completely understandable."

Meyrowitz leaned over from the back seat and stared concernedly at Genelli. "You really feeling that bad?"

Genelli felt as if he had lain down in front of a buffalo stampede. He said as much.

Meyrowitz fumbled in his coat pocket, came out with an aspirin tin, opened it, handed Genelli a tablet that was definitely not mere aspirin.

"What's this?"

"Speed," Meyrowitz said. "Nothing really strong. But it'll cut away the fatigue."

Genelli turned around on the seat and looked back at the young agent. "You took one?"

Meyrowitz nodded.

"Take them often?"

"Only when I pull extended duty and can't get the right sleep. You got to watch this stuff. Steady use will kill you. But in an emergency, it's unbeatable."

"You realize these are illegal?" Genelli asked, holding the green tablet between thumb and forefinger.

"You sound like Peterson," Meyrowitz said.

"I do?"

"Yeah."

Genelli worked up a mouthful of saliva, popped the pill into his mouth, and swallowed it without benefit of water. A few minutes later, he said, "Hey, can it really work this fast?"

Meyrowitz and Plover laughed. Apparently, the driver was no stranger to the pills. Meyrowitz said, "Football and baseball players use them all the time, for quick pickup in a game."

They followed Ashe and Packer as Ashe and Packer followed Ilya Zaitsev.

As they neared Princeton, Genelli said, "Do these things have a psychological effect on you? Do they make you feel paranoid?"

"No," Meyrowitz said.

"Then the idea I just had doesn't come from the speed." He reached over the back of the seat and tapped the shotgun braced there. "I think we may need more than our handguns. You better drop a couple of shells into that."

Meyrowitz nodded. "With a man like Dunio and with someone as disturbed as Douglas Powell, it's not paranoid to be prepared." He unclipped the shotgun and hunted the shells for it.

JANUARY 3

The Decisions

30.

January 3—12:10 A.M.

Lee listened with morbid fascination as Doug Powell explained what would be done with the magnetic tapes and why. It was an *eerie* experience. He was watching an old friend who had changed so much inside that he was now only physically familiar. It was, Lee thought, almost like one of those science fiction movies in which an alien takes over the mind of a human being, casts out and destroys the real person, and hides within the human shell. Doug Powell was filled up with something alien and cold. It was revealed in his dark-ringed eyes, in his strained voice—and, of course, in the madness which he spoke.

"You see why we had to come out here," Powell said. "I had to get out of New York yesterday, because I knew the FBI would be onto me by then. That's why I needed a partner, someone to stay in New York and take care of the ransom collection. I also knew that before yesterday was through, there'd be a warrant out for my arrest. And there is. If you had listened to the radio on your drive out, you'd have heard it. My face is on television screens . . . I couldn't risk going anywhere public just now. So this place is perfect."

"But how can you *ever* leave?" Carrie asked. "Your face will still be known tomorrow and the day after that."

"I'll cut some logs, build a fire in one of the fireplaces, and stay here for ten days or two weeks," Powell said. He was breathless. "They won't think to look here. Why should they? In two weeks, I can pretty well grow a mustache. I can shave my head. It'll be a simple matter to change my appearance enough to get across into Canada two weeks from now, because by then they won't be as watchful. By then, they'll think I've already left the country."

Lee said, "We agreed from the start that those tapes were never to be passed to a foreign agent."

"I lied," Powell said. He smiled, as if charmed by his own audacity. Then, in one of those sudden changes of mood, the amusement degenerated into an hysterical, mirthless laugh.

The gun wavered in his hand. But he did not move it away from them far enough or long enough for Lee to make a move.

"Look," Lee said, "if you mail those tapes back to the Pentagon, like we planned, the worst of the heat will be off. Things will cool down, and you'll have at least *some* chance of starting a new life with those papers Dunio brought for you. But if you turn the tapes over to this Russian friend of yours, the government's never going to stop hunting for you with everything they've got. And they'll find you even if you try to live under another name."

"I don't care," Powell said.

At that moment Lee saw the madness was compounded by fanaticism, and he knew that he had lost the argument. Powell could not be persuaded to change his mind.

Carrie said, "Doug, no matter what your father may have done to you, does he really deserve—"

"He deserves everything!" Powell said fiercely, his face twisting into a satanic mask. "Because of him, I spent a year over there in that hell hole. Because of him and his need to prove his patriotism to his friends in the Army, I spent twelve months scrambling to stay alive. I spent twelve months living in filthy barracks, living in worse when we were in the field. Because of him, I watched my friends die. And I had to kill when I didn't for God's sake *want* to kill, because it was kill or be killed. He sent me to that stinking, death-infested place, and he's going to pay for it."

"Nobody liked it over there," Lee said. "I sure as hell didn't. But there are limits to the revenge you can take, Doug."

"There aren't any limits to *my* revenge," Powell said hotly. His eyes were growing wilder by the moment.

Lee saw that Doug's vicious hatred of his father was not based solely on Vietnam. The roots of it went deeper.

"By the time I was twelve," Powell said, "I hated the old bastard so much I tried to kill him. He was teaching me to hunt, to use a bitty little .22 rifle. I shot him in the chest. Pretended it was an accident. He wasn't hurt bad at all, and for a while I was sorry." He was losing control, rambling feverishly. "But when I got a little older, I understood that killing him was too easy. It was too easy for him. The best revenge is a long and lasting one, a slow revenge."

If the roots of his hatred lay deep, then so did the seeds of his madness. For the first time Lee began to realize that the courage Doug had shown in battle was actually the manic risk-taking of an unbalanced man.

Carrie said, "You're asking everyone else in this country to pay a hell of a steep price just so you can get even with your old man. You realize that?"

"I don't *care* if the whole ship sinks," Powell said. "Just so the general is on it when it goes down."

From that point on he raved at the edge of incoherency. His eyes were too wide, and his voice tended to slur as if he had drunk too much. He waved the gun around carelessly, using it to punctuate his statements.

Lee tried to excite him even further, to distract him. "Don't you realize, Doug, that if the FBI knows it's you they're after, they also know you're a friend of this Zaitsev's? They're probably right behind him. When he shows up here tonight, they'll walk in the door one minute later."

"Impossible," Powell said. "I've only seen him a few times in the last couple of years. And every time, we met in a restaurant which we went to separately. Zaitsev knows what he's doing. He's been obtaining and sending home secret data for two years now."

The gun arm rose.

The revolver was pointing at the ceiling.

Lee pushed off his chair, leapt across the six feet that separated him from Powell, diving for the big man's legs.

A shot exploded.

A bullet struck Lee's shoulder. He had no immediate pain, but he was pitched sideways. Still, he collided with Powell. They went down together.

The Colt was wrenched from Powell's hand, went spinning across the floor and rattled against the base of the refrigerator.

Powell was shouting, cursing.

Realizing that he was no match for the bigger man in a no-holds-barred fight, Lee rolled off Powell. He scrambled desperately across the kitchen floor on his hands and knees, trying to reach the loaded revolver before the other man could come down hard on the back of his neck and either kill him or knock him unconscious.

There was no doubt in his mind that Doug would kill him if he thought that was necessary. This was not the Doug Powell whom he had known in the war. This was an alien masquerading in the human shell, unpredictable and deadly.

Carrie screamed.

Lee's hand fell on the Colt. He grasped it by the barrel, reversed it in his hand, and rolled over onto his back expecting to see Powell looming over him.

Instead, Doug was rushing out of the kitchen door, lugging the suitcase that contained the magnetic tapes.

"Please, Lee, let him go!" Carrie cried. She was still sitting in her chair by the table, rigid with fear. She was, emotionally and intellectually, a remarkably strong woman. But she had never been baptized in violence as he and Powell had been, and she was immobilized by it.

He could not let Powell go as she wanted him to do. If that madman had his way, he would destroy their lives and not just the general's and his own.

Lee pushed to his feet and ran to the door, stepped out into the snow which sprayed up in fine clouds around his feet.

Forty yards away, half-obscured by the blinding snow and the darkness, Doug Powell was running clumsily toward the woods that formed the bulk of the estate. He was lurching like Frankenstein's monster, bowed forward by the weight of the suitcase.

Shoot him?

Lee raised the Colt but hesitated a moment too long. Before he could squeeze off a shot, Powell was in the woods, dodging through the trees, disappearing. Gone . . . Lee tried to content himself with the knowledge that, at such a distance, the Colt would have been no good anyway.

31.

January 3—12:45 A.M.

"You've been shot."

"It's nothing."

"You're bleeding," Carrie said. "You simply can't stay here, bleeding like that."

His left arm from the shoulder to the elbow was hurting badly enough to make him dizzy, but he maintained an unruffled demeanor for her benefit. "The bullet passed straight through," he said. "It didn't hit any blood vessels, or my coat would be soaked. It's a surface wound, a scratch."

"All that blood—"

"Isn't as much as it appears to be," he said. "You're just not used to seeing blood. Look, the wound pretty much cauterized itself from the heat of the bullet. It *can't* be serious."

They were standing in the cold kitchen, in the flickering light of the votive candles, where he had stripped off his coat to let her examine the wound. Now, he was struggling back into the coat. His left arm was getting stiff and painfully difficult to manage, but he tried his best to hide that from her as he jammed it into his coatsleeve. The wound actually *was* minor, and he was not about to let it stop him.

"But what can you *do* here?"

"Find him."

"He's run off."

"No," Lee said. "He's out there in the woods, waiting for us to drive away."

"You can't know that."

"Of course I can. He's out there waiting for this Ilya Zaitsev to show up. Carrie, he's out there *with the tapes.*"

"To hell with saving the country," she said. Her blue eyes caught and held the candle flames. "I just want you to be safe, with me."

"I'm not thinking about saving the country," he said. "At least, not altogether. Carrie, I *know* there'll be federal agents right behind this Russian. But even if there aren't . . . Sooner or later, they're going to catch Doug. In his present state of mind, if he gets nailed, you know they'll break him down. No matter how much or little he meant that promise to keep us out of it, he'd tell them everything. He's too unstable to be trusted."

"And you're going to heal him?" she asked sarcastically. "You think you can talk him out of his madness?"

"No," he said. "I'll have to kill him."

She stared at him as if he had spoken a foreign language that she had not been aware he knew.

"Believe me, you're no more shocked than I am," Lee said.

"Kill him?"

"I didn't even realize, until I said it, what I had in mind." That was true. His stomach had rolled sickeningly when he had heard himself make that commitment to violence. "But he's no longer my friend. Doug's not even remotely the man I knew—or thought I knew. He's dangerous . . . But more than that, he's just as blind to my right to shape my own life as the government has been. He's just one more person who thinks he has the right to design my future and destroy my happiness according to his whim. And I've had enough of that. I've regained some of my self-respect through all of this, and I'm not going to surrender it."

"Won't you lose your self-respect by killing him?" she asked.

"No. As horrible as it may sound, I'm used to killing. In the war, I had to do lots of it. I'm accustomed to slaughter."

"But over there," she said, "you were fighting for your life."

"I am here too," he said.

"Lee . . ."

He finished buttoning his coat, went over to the table where all the cash was piled. "Help me scoop this into the suitcase," he said, nodding at the brown Samsonite bag that Dunio had left them. "You'll take it with you."

"Why can't I stay until you've—gotten rid of him?"

"You have to get our car out of here before the Russian shows up, before the federal men show up."

"But how will you get out of here?" she asked.

"On foot. This place isn't isolated, after all. It's practically in the middle of Princeton." He threw packets of money into the suitcase. "Even if the FBI descends on the estate in droves, I can make it out on foot. The army didn't just teach me to kill. It taught me to move over enemy terrain without being spotted. The darkness and the snow will only help."

"You'll be wanted for murder," she said, finally coming over to help him with the money.

"No." he said. "You heard what Doug said about the warrants that have been issued. They think Dunio was his partner. And they'll be after Dunio for murder." Could they really be having this nightmarish conversation? Didn't it have to be a dream?

"And they'll never get their hands on Dunio. There's no chance of them getting a lead on us through him."

She threw the last of the half million dollars into the case.

He closed the lid, latched it. Lifting the case with his right hand, trying not to make the stiffness of his left arm too obvious, he started for the door.

After a brief hesitation, she followed him out to the rented Ford.

After he had thrown the suitcase full of money onto the back seat of the car, he helped her get in behind the wheel. Leaning in at the open door, snow pummeling his back, he said, "You think you can drive in this stuff?"

Slanting almost horizontally across the night, driven by a hard wind, the snow severely cut visibility. The highway would be a ribbon of ice.

"I've driven in worse," she said, determined to be every bit as tough as he was. "Once I get back out to the turnpike, it'll be easy going."

He kissed her.

When she started the car and raced the sluggish engine, she looked up at him and said, "Lee, he's so big."

"He's not that big."

"Bigger than you are."

"But he doesn't have a gun now," Lee said. "And I do."

"I'm going to be worried sick."

He gave her one last kiss. "Go back to the apartment. In the morning, be sure to go to work as usual. I'll try to get back home tonight. But I might not."

"Lee—"

"Now get the hell out of here before half the police in the world come up the driveway!" He slammed her door and waved her toward the hill that marked the top of the drive.

He watched her leave until the taillights were just a glow in the darkness, diffused by the heavy snow, hidden from him by the down-slanting driveway. Then he walked back through the mounting snow to the kitchen, where he located both Colt Diamondbacks and loaded them. One was completely empty, and the other needed a bullet to replace the one Powell had fired at him.

He gingerly touched his left shoulder. It was less sore than it was numb. It would be a problem if Powell managed to jump him out there.

Leaving the candles to gutter behind him, he set out toward that spot at the perimeter of the woods where Powell had disappeared.

32.

January 3—1:00 A.M.

He stretched out in the snow and looked down at the trail just eight feet below. This is where it would happen, then. It was within his power to choose the spot, and he liked this place.

He knew that Lee would come after him.

In the kitchen, when they had both been sprawled on the floor, Powell had seen that there was no chance for him to reach the Colt before Lee did. The only thing he could do was grab the tapes and run, secure in the knowledge that Lee would follow him. He had gained time to prepare himself, had taken the advantage. When Lee came into the woods, he would be entering Powell's territory, land which Powell had walked earlier and knew well. Then, he would jump Lee and get the Colt and use it.

It was just terrible how things had deteriorated between them. After all, he had *promised* Lee that he would keep him safe all the way through this affair. And now he was going to have to break that promise. Of course, Lee had forced him to this. Why did Lee have to change sides? Why did he have to turn and join the others, side with the general? They could have done so much together. Look at what they had pulled off already!

But Lee couldn't or wouldn't understand . . .

Justice had to be done and the general had to suffer and sweet Loretta had to suffer because she was a drunkard and because she was a slave to the general. And when it came to that, the whole damn ugly world had to suffer and crumble and fall apart so that something new and better could rise from the rubble . . . The country had to suffer for making him kill, for teaching him to kill, for all the nightmare times he had seen his own bullets blast the brains out of a little yellow man who had wanted to blast *his* brains out . . . They couldn't stop short at taking the ransom and returning the tapes, but had to strike deep into the guts of the country and tear open the guts of the country and tear open the general and tear open Loretta. Justice had to be done, because it *should* have been done years ago when he was twelve years old and when he had not succeeded in killing the old bastard . . .

Because he did not grasp that fundamental truth, Lee Ackridge would have to go, no matter what they might have been to each other in the past. Ackridge was standing between Powell and the justice which Powell longed to administer.

Kill Ackridge.

It was down to that, because Powell knew that Ackridge would look at it the same way. He *should* be able to predict the other man's response. After all, they had been educated in the same school of strategy and mayhem, hadn't they? They had learned violence from the same teacher.

It was risky. If he could predict Lee's behavior, then Lee could also predict his. That was a chance he had to take. He did not mind. The important thing was ruining the general. Escape was not important at all, by comparison. Any risk was necessary.

So . . . It was only a question of who got the jump on whom. And Powell had the advantage of surprise.

He shivered as the snow melted under him and soaked into his clothes and chilled his flesh. Despite the discomfort, he smiled at the darkness.

January 3—1:10 A.M.

Without much trouble, Lee found the path that Powell had used. Although the snow was quickly sifting over them, there were footprints which he could see even in the meager light of the storm.

After a dozen steps, he stopped and removed the snow-filmed, long-haired wig and stuffed it in his coat pocket. Then he went on.

A hundred feet in from the edge of the trees, the land began to slope and become treacherous. Because there were only a few scattered pines here and no leaves on the other varieties of trees, the snow was accumulating in the forest almost as deeply as it was out on the open ground. White, powdery flakes as soft and seemingly as dry as talcum powder mounted over the tops of his shoes and greased the earth beneath him.

He moved with acquired stealth. The New Jersey woods in winter were far different from the steamy jungles and arid plains of Southeast Asia. Yet he could easily apply the things the Army had taught him. He thought out his alternatives before he took each step, and he moved with quiet deliberation.

He was plagued by the irrational fear that Doug Powell was coming up behind him, that Powell had been very close to him ever since he had set foot in the forest, that Powell was just playing some sort of game, toying with him. Several times, he was so overwhelmed with this particular vision that he turned quickly and looked back the way he had come, but he was always alone.

Wind moaned through the bare black branches on all sides of him, made wooden tuning forks out of them, and filled the night with scores of banshee cries.

Snowflakes iced his hair, tickled his ears and nostrils. They crusted his coat and trousers and somehow found their way around his tightly buttoned coat collar.

The pathway dropped more precipitously now, and the land began to rise on the right of it until an eight- or nine-foot bluff sheltered him from the worst of the wind and the stinging curtain of snow.

For a moment, as he turned a bend in the path, he was thankful for this respite. And then he saw that there were no more footprints on the virgin snow ahead, and he discovered that it was here where Powell had chosen to wait for him.

Damn!

He whirled around.

Even as Lee was turning, Powell came to his feet atop the bluff, a nightmare creature rising as if he had been folded up in the forest sod. In one fluid movement he stepped to the brink and launched himself out and down.

Lee raised the gun in his right hand.

Powell struck him with such force that the gun went flying and Lee collapsed backwards into the snow. The breath was knocked out of him.

Together, he and Powell rolled over and over down the path, underbrush whipping at them. Lee felt himself snared, then held by a patch of blackberry brambles.

The pain in his left shoulder blossomed, flowered with petals of fire that burned fiercely. The cauterized scar where the bullet had grazed him earlier in the night now broke open in the fall. He could feel warm blood trickling down his arm and soaking into the inside of his coatsleeve. It was such an intense pain that fanned out from the bleeding wound that he did not want to move. He wanted only to lay very still and hope that it would gradually recede.

But Powell would have the advantage and—Where *was* Powell?

Lee suddenly realized that he had been stunned long enough for the other man to have throttled him. Yet he was alive. Why?

He struggled to a sitting position and saw Powell stooping over to pick up the Colt Diamondback from the snow, twenty feet up the narrow path.

Powell was laughing.

With considerable agony, Lee managed to get to his knees and take the remaining revolver from his coat pocket. He held it in both hands. "Doug," he said softly.

Grinning, the other man rose and turned. He shot once, but wildly.

Lee shot him once in the groin, once in the stomach, once in the chest, and once in the neck. Two shots missed the target altogether.

In the last seconds of life, as he was slammed backwards by the bullets, Powell was clearly surprised that Lee had thought to bring both revolvers. The surprise was brief. In the ghostly radiance of the snow, which only dimly illuminated his long face, he lost all expression. He settled down in the snow in a loose heap, and he died.

The two Bureau cars had stopped on the snow-clogged highway by the turnoff which Ilya Zaitsev had taken, giving the Russian plenty of time to get up to the house on the hill and make contact with Powell. If, indeed, it was Powell he had come all this way in a snowstorm to see.

"O.K.," Genelli said into the microphone after three or four minutes had elapsed. "Let's go get them."

"Right," Ashe said from the car in front. "But Packer says you better keep your distance. The driveway's long and steep and pretty damn snowy. We'll be doing some sliding on the way up."

"Go slide," Genelli said.

Agent Packer put his car in gear and led the way past a mailbox labeled JAMISON, and on up the slippery lane where barren elm trees thrust craggy branches out from the high banks on both sides. The tires whined and spun. The two big engines roared insistently and forced the cars ahead inch by stubborn inch.

When they finally came out on top and pulled in by the big white house, Ilya Zaitsev was standing by his car watching them. He waved at them as if they were friends for whom he'd been waiting.

"Shotgun?" Genelli asked Meyrowitz.

"Ready."

They piled out of the car and moved in on Zaitsev who stopped waving and smiling. He said, "Oh, no."

"FBI," Genelli said, not bothering to produce identification.

Zaitsev was stunned. He was a tall, overweight man with a broad face and heavy jowls and tiny eyes that were now the very essence of fear.

"Where are the others?" Genelli demanded.

"They are not here," Zaitsev said.

Genelli pushed him up against the car, knocking off his hat which the wind caught and blew away. "Where are the others?" he demanded again. "Where's Powell?"

Zaitsev sighed as he realized the full scope of their knowledge. "I told the truth. I came, looked inside, and found no one. And please do not push me around. I would remind you of the International Convention on Diplomatic Immunity."

Genelli was about to push him around some more when six shots boomed from the woods nearly a hundred yards distant.

"Plover," Genelli said, "watch this man."

"Yes, sir."

"Packer, you watch the house. Ashe and Meyrowitz, come with me."

He headed across the lawn toward the trees, in the direction from which the shots had come.

Carrying the heavy suitcase full of mag tapes, Lee Ackridge struggled down from the small bluff and returned to Powell's body. He dropped the bag in the bloodied snow.

He was cold and hungry and dizzy, but not miserable. He was oddly satisfied and more content than he had been since before he'd gone to Asia.

He had just recovered his breath when the men began to call down from the edge of the woods.

"Powell! Dunio!"

He looked up that way and saw nothing.

"We're FBI agents!" one of the voices called again. "We know what the two of you have done. There's no way you can escape us for good, even if you manage to slip out of these woods tonight. Do the smart thing. Come on up here. Let us take you in."

Smiling, Lee opened the suitcase and emptied the tapes over Powell's body. Then, turning away as the agents above continued to call out, he went to the bottom of the hill and across a shallow glen. There, he found a creek no more than six feet wide and two feet deep. Most of it was frozen, but the center was cut by a channel of dark, babbling water. He trudged out into the stream, looked north and south, turned south. The water was icy, numbing his feet and calves. He walked a hundred yards, then left the stream, taking long steps and turning after each one to smooth over the snow as best he could.

He came to a rail fence that separated the Jamison property from another. Clambering over it, he stumbled and almost fell when he came down on the other side.

He rested a moment.

The voices were more distant now, almost unintelligible.

The wind was gentling down, but the snow was falling faster than ever. There were four inches on the ground now. At this rate, by dawn, there would be at least four more.

He had to move on. He could freeze here.

Before the storm stranded him in Princeton, he had to find a way out. In this area, he was easy pickings for the FBI.

Staggering slightly, he continued on through another arm of the woods until he came into the rear lawn of a house as impressive as the Jamisons' place had been. He looked at the large black windows, saw no lights at all and no movement of drapes which might have indicated the presence of an insomniac who was sitting up watching the snow fall.

He crossed the yard, passed the side of the house, and went out to a regular upper-middle class residential street. There were no more estates here, but a number of fine-looking homes.

On both sides of the street, a few cars were parked at widely spaced intervals by the curbs. Watching from the shadows at the corner of one house, he satisfied himself that the street was deserted. Shaking from exhaustion and exposure to extreme cold, he went up one side of the block and down the other until he found a car with its doors unlocked. Murmuring thanks to the careless owner, he slid in behind the wheel and pulled the door shut.

A few minutes later, when he could feel his heartbeat slowing, he reached under the dashboard with his good right hand and pulled down a bath of wires. Using both hands, he found the two he wanted.

Then vertigo claimed him, and he passed out at the bottom of a long, dizzy spiral.

33.

January 3—1:50 A.M.

Genelli stood over Douglas Powell's corpse while Meyrowitz knelt beside it and carefully put the tapes back into the suitcase. "All of them accounted for?"

"Six," Meyrowitz said. He looked up, perplexed. "Did Dunio shoot him? And why did he just leave the tapes here?"

Genelli thought about it a moment. "Dunio sounds like a shrewd and practical capitalist. He probably didn't realize until today that Powell intended to pass the tapes to the Russians whether or not the ransom was paid. Dunio could see the folly of that sort of deal. So he killed Powell. And he left the tapes here, because he knew we'd find them."

Meyrowitz stood up. "Now?"

"Now we go after Dunio," Genelli said, looking down into the lightless woods. He turned to Ashe. "Go back to the house. Use the radio to get the state police. And the closest Bureau field office. We're going to have to cordon off the entire area." As Ashe struggled up the slope, Genelli said, "Come on, Meyrowitz, let's do a little foot work."

Together, revolvers in hand, they went down the path, following the well-delineated footsteps in the snow.

"Still the plow horse," Meyrowitz said.

"What else is there to do?"

When Lee Ackridge came to, he did not know how long he had been unconscious. All he knew was that he had lost precious minutes and that he dared not delay any longer. He felt sick to his stomach, and he wanted nothing but to lie down and sleep. Instead, he found the right wires again and stroked them together as he pumped the accelerator.

The car, a two-year-old Pontiac, coughed.

He stroked the wires, tramped the gas to the floor.

The engine caught with a roar.

He sat up, closed his eyes a moment, opened them with a start as he felt himself sliding toward an exhausted sleep.

He opened the door, got out of the car, scooped up snow and rubbed it in his face. He let some of it melt in his hands and drank the cold slush.

When he got back into the Pontiac, he was pretty certain that he could take the car the whole way into New York and abandon it there before it was missed. The only problem was learning how to drive one-handed in the middle of a major snowstorm. And he would have to go by back roads and avoid the inevitable roadblock on the turnpike and other superhighways. However, considering what he had been through during these last three or four years, he knew that he could make it. It was cake.

Genelli and Meyrowitz stood at the edge of the creek where the footprints disappeared.

"Shine your light on the other bank," Genelli said.

Meyrowitz did.

There were no prints over there.

"He went up or down, walking in the water," Genelli said. "And you know what?"

"What?" Meyrowitz asked, blinking snow out of his eyes.

"I'll bet you won't find where he came out."

"Why?"

"Because he knows what he's doing," Genelli said.

"Then we quit?"

"Can't quit," Genelli said. "We're going to be thrashing around out here this time tomorrow night. Peterson will see to that."

Meyrowitz sighed and started out onto the ice.

"Wait," Genelli said.

The younger agent looked back.

"After this is over," Genelli said, "no more tracking down pornographers and investigating the Quaker peace movement while the murder rate soars like my blood pressure . . . Why the hell don't we both get out of it, Meyrowitz? You know this is going to be the last interesting case you'll see in years . . . And worse yet, it wasn't anything as satisfying as it should have been. These days, the outrageous has become commonplace." He looked down at the ice that was glittering fantastically under the beam of Meyrowitz's flashlight. "Even your villains aren't as satisfying as they once were. They're just confused people. Like everyone else. Look at Powell, for example." He frowned. "Yeah, you have to get out of it with me."

"What would I do?" Meyrowitz asked.

"Maybe we could go into business together," Genelli said.

"Business?"

"Start our own detective agency."

Meyrowitz thought that was really funny. "Sam Spadowitz and Mike Hammerelli, you mean?"

"Something like that," Genelli said. He walked out onto the ice and stepped into the cold water which surged to his knees. He shuddered. Strangely for him, he was not really thinking much about the remaining threads to be tied up in this investigation. Instead, he was recalling the dream that he had been having when Peterson had woke him and assigned him to the case. It had been a little vision of a family reunion . . .

"Where would we start an agency of our own?" Meyrowitz asked as he stepped into the water beside Genelli.

"Anywhere," Genelli said. He thought about the family reunion. It was probably too late for him to have a family. But he could find *someone.* Perhaps the reason he'd never gotten really close to the women he slept with was because he never *tried* to love and know them. It was time to try. It had taken him twenty years to realize that it was not so much *what* you did with your life, but how happy you made someone else in the living of it.

"If we started an agency of our own in Washington," Meyrowitz said, "do you think we could really make a living at it?"

"Well, maybe we wouldn't earn as much at first as we're earning now in the Bureau. But money isn't the only criterion. No matter how much we took in, we'd be living better than we are now."

"Let's think about it," Meyrowitz said.

"Sure," Genelli said.

Meyrowitz went south in the creek.

Genelli went north.

Epilogue

Harold Dunio and his bodyguard were waiting at the prearranged corner table in the hotel bar in Toronto. Dunio was drinking Scotch neat, while his bodyguard was drinking Coca-Cola on the rocks. They were the only customers in the place at three in the afternoon.

Lee sat down in one of the black leather captain's chairs, ordered bourbon, and waited until it had been brought before he said anything. "I really didn't expect you to show up."

"I always keep my commitments," Dunio said somewhat indignantly.

"But you know about Doug?"

"Sure," Dunio said. "So I didn't bring his cut." He grinned, picked up his cigar and puffed on it. "Brought yours, though."

The tall, handsome bodyguard took a plain white envelope from his pocket and handed it to Lee.

"I figured you didn't need any cash," Dunio said. "Not with what I gave you two weeks ago."

Trembling slightly, Lee opened the envelope and thumbed through the contents. Twenty-two bank checks drawn for one hundred thousand dollars each. And one check for fifty thousand. He closed the envelope and put it in his jacket pocket.

"Be careful how you spend it," Dunio said.

"For the next few years," Lee said, "I won't touch more than three or four thousand of it, supplement my regular income. By then, I can find ways to clean it."

"There's a telephone number in that envelope," Dunio said. "If you ever need an art dealer again, you can get hold of me through a friend at that number."

"I'll be sure to do that," Lee said.

They finished their drinks in silence, then got up and walked out of the bar. In the lobby Lee shook hands with Dunio, then stood and watched as they left the hotel and climbed into a black Cadillac parked out front. When they pulled away, Lee patted the envelope in his pocket and then went upstairs to the room to make love to Carrie.

It was a good day.